SAVE THE LAST DANCE FOR ME

by Cora Lee

This is a work of fiction. Names, characters, businesses, places, events, and incidents are either the products of the author's imagination or used in a fictitious manner.

No part of this book was created with the use of AI. It is was produced through the hard work and creativity of the author, editor, and cover designer.

Hymn to Aphrodite by Sappho, translated into English by Ambrose Philips as *A Hymn to Venus*

Editing by Jude Simms.

Cover by Erin Dameron-Hill at EDH Professionals.

ISBN 978-1-944477-22-6

Published by More Than Words Press.

For my grandmothers, Ardis and Joanne, who
passed down to me their love of reading.

Prologue

November 1812

ℬENEDICT GREY SAT AS CLOSE to the fire in his library as he could without singeing the book—*Remarks on the Antiquities of Rome and Its Environs: Being a Classical and Topographical Survey of the Ruins of that Celebrated City*—in his lap. It was good to be in his own home again, to sleep in his own soft bed, to eat his favorite foods. To wash in the morning and know that he would not be covered in dust inside of an hour.

But after spending the larger part of six years in Greece, London was *cold*.

There was a knock at the door and, at Benedict's easy "enter", his butler stepped into the room. "The Marquess of Whitby to see you, sir."

"It's deuced dark in here, Benedict," Whitby proclaimed, brushing past the butler and heading for a big wing chair opposite his host. "Why are all the curtains closed?"

Benedict's reply—and nod to the retreating butler—was matter-of-fact. "To keep the heat in."

Whitby laughed. "Of course! You must be positively freezing. Why on earth did you come back to England in November of all months?"

"I came back with the last load of cargo. It was either sail with it, or wait until the winter storms had passed. With two wars on, I didn't want to become stranded in a foreign country."

"Wish you'd stayed in Athens, now, don't you?"

Whitby was grinning. Benedict found himself rubbing his arms and grinning back. "Absolutely."

"Have you been to see Elgin yet?"

Benedict sobered somewhat at the mention of his patron. "I have—it was his endeavor after all. His lordship bore the expenses, he has a right to hear the particulars first hand."

"But you didn't call on any of your family?"

Benedict shifted in his chair. "I wanted a few days to recover first."

"And to hide, eh?"

Benedict ignored the jibe. Instead, he rose from his chair and placed a marker in his book, stroking a finger gently over the cover as he set the volume on his desk.

He strode toward the sideboard to pour drinks. "What are you doing in Town? I thought you were rusticating in the country with your flock of daughters."

"It's my 'flock of daughters' that brings me here."

Benedict heard the sudden seriousness in Whitby's voice and turned at once. "Is everything well with the girls?"

"Oh, they're hale and hearty. All aflutter about dresses and bonnets and such, I imagine. They're going to visit my wife's sister for a month, and were twittering about what to pack when I departed."

Benedict turned back to the sideboard, feeling his shoulders relax as he poured a clear liquid into two glasses. "What do you need from me, then?"

"Two things. First, my wife is holding a house party while the girls are away to celebrate Christmas and your safe return."

Benedict returned to his place by the fire, handing a glass to his cousin. "Try this—I brought it back with me. And I'll not think you a coward for sipping it."

Whitby took the glass and sniffed at it. "Smells like the biscuits Cook makes on special occasions."

"*Stin uyeia sou.*" At his cousin's blank look, Benedict translated his words. "To your health."

Whitby sniffed again, then tossed back the entire glass.

And came up coughing.

Benedict was obliged to get up and pound his cousin on the back, receiving a scowl for his trouble.

"What the hell is this?"

"It's called ouzo. The Greeks drink it regularly."

"Well the English do not. You should have warned me of its potency—*actually* warned me, instead of provoking me like that."

Benedict resumed his seat, arching an eyebrow at his cousin. "You let your wife give a house party for me."

"*Let* her? You know better than that."

Benedict allowed a small smile to form on his lips. If any wife had charge of her husband, it was certainly Lady Whitby.

"Well, we're even now. What was the second thing?"

"What?"

"You said there were two things you needed of me. The first was the house party—which I haven't yet agreed to. What is the second thing?"

Whitby sat forward in his chair, leaning his forearms against his thighs. "Take a drink of that ouzo first."

Benedict did as instructed before replying. "Please don't tell me you want me to squire around some silly girl at this house party."

"Worse," Whitby said slowly. "I need you to get married."

Benedict looked at his cousin for a long moment, trying to analyze his expression in the dim light of the fire. Was he joking?

"And produce an heir."

He had to be joking. Not that Benedict didn't have a fondness for women. Perhaps he had a bit less experience with them than other men of eight-and-twenty years, but he'd enjoyed every moment of what he'd had.

Before a man could marry a woman, though, he had to first find one of the right class and breeding, the right family and wealth. Then he had to court her.

"Truly, Benedict. I wouldn't ask if it was not of the utmost importance."

Benedict downed the rest of his ouzo in one swallow.

"Why?"

Whitby sat back, hands still resting on his thighs. "To secure the succession."

"Of course."

A great, long sigh whooshed out of the marquess. "You're my heir—and the last Grey male. You had to know this was coming."

"Eventually, yes. But not three days after I returned to London. Bloody hell, Whitby, I've been gone for most of the last six years—you couldn't wait a few more days?"

"I thought you could use as much warning as possible."

Benedict pressed his lips together in a tight line. "Your lady wife is planning more than just a house party."

Whitby nodded, his eyes—the same hazel as Benedict's—flicking toward the fire. "She's...she's been having a bad time of it these last months." He stopped and drew in a deep breath, as if steeling himself for the worst. "She can't have any more children."

"Why not?" His mother would likely have elbowed him in the ribs for such a lack of delicacy, but Benedict ignored the thought.

Whitby's eyes dropped from the fire to the floor. "She's past her childbearing years. She's seen physicians and midwives, consulted apothecaries. They all say the same thing."

"She's not that old, is she?"

"I didn't think so—my mother bore her last child when she was nigh on five-and-forty, and Lady Whitby has more than a few years to go before she reaches that milestone. But our youngest is nearly six now, and there's not been even a hint of another babe since. She won't say it aloud, but I can see it all over her face—she feels old and useless. She gave me seven daughters, but doesn't think that's good enough."

"I'm...sorry." Benedict was sure that was not the correct sentiment to express, but he didn't know what else to say.

"Of course, having you as my heir helps. We both know you'll do the title honor when your turn comes."

Understanding dawned. "And now Lady Whitby can turn her attention to my matrimonial prospects."

Whitby's eyes shifted back to his cousin. "It's cheered her up considerably, planning this house party and dreaming up eligible ladies for you to meet."

Benedict realized he was still holding his empty ouzo glass and set it down on the hearth at his feet. "She feels useful again."

"Exactly so."

A long silence stretched between the two men. Benedict took his turn staring at the fire, but he could feel his cousin's eyes on him. He knew Whitby wanted him to agree to the whole scheme, to attend the house party with pleasure and throw himself into a search for a suitable wife.

Benedict, however, knew what he was like around the Society set—or anyone outside his fellow antiquarians.

He bored them to tears.

Each time he had returned home during the expedition to Greece had been a disaster. Once, his arrival had coincided with the height of the Season, and his mother had dragged him to every entertainment she'd been invited to. He'd been polite, of course, and had tried to make conversation with the countless people she'd introduced him to. But when they had asked him breathless questions about his time in Athens, he had inevitably responded with the condition and significance of items recovered during the previous months. When people had asked his opinion of the war against Napoleon, Benedict's reaction had been to condemn it—if Britain had not embroiled herself in armed conflict, he might be able to travel safely to Italy and work on the excavation of Pompeii.

After that, few people had asked him questions. In fact, few people had spoken to him much at all.

But he couldn't bring himself to damage Lady Whitby's delicate mental state. Given his cousin's news and the way in which he'd deliver it, Benedict suspected that if he rebuffed the marchioness's matchmaking machinations she'd sink into a deep depression. And if he could prevent that, or lessen its severity in any way, he was certainly willing to try.

But surely he needn't submit to *all* her machinations.

"Well, I won't deprive her of her house party, then." Benedict paused, making sure to catch Whitby's gaze and hold it. "And I will allow that, under the circumstances, it's time I started looking for a wife. But how and when I do so will be *my* decision."

"That's fair." Whitby was nodding his head agreeably. "A good start, at least."

"Not a start, cousin. That's my line in the sand. You and I have always been like brothers, despite the difference in our ages, and I love your wife like my own sister. But I'll not be dictated to on the matter of *my* wife and the mother of my children."

"Sure, sure. You'll find the right woman. I have no doubt."

There was a slight slur to Whitby's words, and Benedict looked more closely at his cousin. His cheeks were flushed pink, his mouth pulled into a lazy smile.

Benedict grinned, leaning against the high back of his chair. While he was accustomed to Greece's favorite alcohol, Whitby was clearly not. He wondered briefly if he might extract other promises from the marquess, but discarded the notion. It would be dishonorable to attempt such a thing. And Whitby would never do so himself.

Instead, Benedict simply continued the conversation, albeit in a slightly more relaxed tone. "I'm surprised you didn't suggest one of your daughters for me."

Whitby waved a hand at his cousin. "No, not my girls. They're sweet creatures, but flighty...and no sign that any of 'em will settle down. Besides, the oldest is only seventeen—would you want to be leg-shackled to a flighty girl of seventeen?"

Benedict felt himself wince at the thought. "No, I would not. And I thank you for taking that into consideration."

"But there will be a multitude of other ladies for you to look over. Best decide what kind of girl you *do* want."

"I suppose I must," Benedict answered, slumping down in his chair. "And what kind of girl might want me."

"Oh, that's easy," Whitby grinned. "You're the grandson of a marquess, heir to a venerable old title...and you've got some money in your own right. The matchmaking mamas will be pounding down your door!"

Benedict slouched further in his chair. "Perhaps I'll tell them I expect my wife to accompany me on future digs."

Whitby laughed. "That would put off the title hunters!"

And pretty much every other lady of the *ton.* Which would break Lady Whitby's heart, and put an end to the Grey line.

Blast it.

Well, there was no turning back now. "I've never been to a house party, cousin. Tell me how it's going to go, and what I must do."

Chapter 1

April 1813

ℬENEDICT HAD LITERALLY BACKED HIMSELF into a corner.

He felt the ballroom wall bump solidly against his shoulder and discovered he was more than a little relieved. At least no one could ambush him from behind.

No one was approaching from the front, though, either. Here he was with hundreds of people at the first great entertainment of the Season, and even the chaperones and spinsters wanted little to do with him.

Not that he blamed them. Most of the *ton* had heard the details of Whitby's Christmas house party by now. They'd know how tongue-tied and awkward Benedict had been, even with the maids when he'd had occasion to speak to one. They'd know how his face had gone distinctly red whenever his turn came at charades, and how he'd inadvertently insulted Whitby's neighbor with what turned out to be a very politically charged remark. Everyone who cared to listen to the gossip would know that he'd given up after that, and spent the remainder of the party in the library, hiding away where he could neither inflict nor receive further harm.

Not that his cowardice had put Lady Whitby off. She'd been upset, of course. But here in her own ballroom with the crème of the *beau monde* swirling all around her, Lady Whitby was in her element. In fact, she was more determined than ever to find him a suitable wife, making lists of eligible young widows and new debutantes, practically following him around Town as he attempted to go about his business.

And she'd just spotted him.

He watched with a sort of detached fascination as she homed in on him from across the room like a hound after a stag. Even amid the bustle and noise of the crowd, the music of the orchestra, and the myriad of people stopping to speak with her, she remained focused on Benedict. Perhaps if he stayed completely still—

"Oh!" a female voice cried. A weight came down on his foot as the rustle of fabric swept against his legs. His arms reached out instinctively and caught hold of a soft form in a white gown dotted with silver embroidery.

"Thank you, sir," the voice said, a little breathless as its owner attempted to right herself. One pale hand braced itself against the lapel of his black evening coat while the other found his shoulder. A curl of dark hair brushed against his cheek. "My dance partner seems rather too vigorous this evening."

"Honoria?"

Long-lashed lids lifted to reveal a pair of eyes as dark as her hair, and her mouth curved into a surprised smile. "Benedict! I didn't know you'd be here tonight."

Aware that heads were turning their way, he removed his arms from her waist and clasped her hands in his, extracting them from his body with as much subtlety as he could manage.

"Isn't everybody here?"

Her gloved hands slipped from his and he felt a pang of regret. Once upon a time a reunion between the two of them would have included a warm—and deliberate—embrace. They were in public, though, and whatever their relationship had previously been, he reminded himself that it would hardly be the same after his years spent abroad.

Her gaze dropped to his waistcoat—silver silk with little leaves embroidered on it, made especially for this ball—and she smoothed her hands over her skirt, making the silver threads catch the light from the chandeliers above. "No one would miss the marchioness's Black and White Ball, of course. But you were never one for society affairs." Her eyes shifted back to his. "Is that why you're over here in the corner? Do you think to hide from the revelry rather than participate in it?"

Well, at least her directness hadn't changed. "As it happened, you're lucky I was here in this particular corner. If I had been out among the revelers, you would have fallen."

Honoria glanced around and Benedict followed suit, noting that people had turned back to their previous activities—except for Lady Whitby. She had resumed her course and was headed directly for him.

"Then for once I appreciate your wallflower ways." She grinned up at him. "You have saved me from what surely would have been the *on dit* of the week."

"Judging by what I saw on the terrace earlier, you would not have even been the *on dit* of the evening. But you could repay an act of gallantry with one of your own."

"What would you have me do?"

He took her hand and laid it on his sleeve. "Walk with me and pretend you enjoy my company."

Lady Honoria Maitland strolled through the ballroom beside her old friend, hoping this was the turning point she'd been waiting for all evening. She'd run into one aggravation after another since the moment she arrived. The shawl she'd worn against the chilly spring night had caught on the door latch of the carriage and torn. Her stepmother had introduced her to two gentlemen whose acquaintance she had previously made but desperately wished she hadn't. She'd accepted a third gentleman's request for a dance hoping to escape the first two, and nearly ended up face down on the floor.

But then Benedict Grey had caught her, and the evening began to show some promise. It had been months and months since they'd even seen each other, and so much longer since they'd had a real conversation. Perhaps that could be remedied tonight.

"Of course I will walk with you. Perhaps we can evade my dance partner—I have no desire to return to his ministrations. And I always enjoy your company."

They strolled away from his corner refuge with all the dignity of visiting royalty. Or at least Honoria did—spine straight, shoulders back, chin up. Benedict's eyes darted around the room as if he was plotting his escape.

Perhaps he was.

But his voice was calm when he spoke again. "Where shall we walk?"

"Let's take a turn about the room for a start." She grinned. "Because if the activities you witnessed on the terrace are still in progress, we'll want to avoid going there."

Benedict merely nodded, so she wracked her brain for another option and decided that a little forwardness would not go amiss with this man. At least, it never had before. "Dancing is also a good way to occupy one's time at a ball."

He cringed visibly. "You want to dance?"

"I love to dance, you know that." Her mouth and feet both paused while she looked more closely at her friend. His shoulders were slightly hunched as he halted beside her, and she could just make out a red tint creeping into his cheeks from beneath his snow white cravat. "Or, you used to know that. Have you forgotten all those afternoons we practiced together when we were young?"

"The afternoons I remember well." He took a half step closer to her and bent his head toward hers. "It's the steps I've forgotten."

"Truly?"

Benedict's eyes trailed down toward his shoes. "Yes, well, there isn't much call for a reel or a quadrille in the middle of an ancient ruin, is there?"

"I suppose not. "Honoria's mouth curved into a slow smile as an idea popped into her head. "But if you're in Town to stay, you'll need to re-acquire that skill."

She must have looked more mischievous than she realized because he straightened abruptly. "You sound like Lady Whitby."

"Is she the one you were hiding from?"

"I was *not* hiding."

The couple nearest them turned for a moment, and Honoria offered what she hoped was an apologetic look before tugging Benedict into motion. "Very well, you weren't hiding. But is the lady in question acting...rather too zealously for your taste?"

"That would be the most polite way to describe her efforts, yes." They walked along without speaking for a few paces before Benedict inched closer again. "What do you know about it?"

Honoria patted his sleeve. "I know only what news your mother has passed along to my stepmother, and that mainly consisted of your continued health and bachelorhood."

His gaze snapped to hers as if he'd been startled by her words. When he coughed and forced a smile, she knew she'd caught him out.

"Ah, so that's what Lady Whitby is after. She wants to see you wed."

"'To a woman of good breeding, with a pretty face and a head for details'," he quoted in an unnaturally high voice. He cleared his throat and resumed his own tenor. "The succession must be secured, of course."

Honoria grimaced, her gaze drifting toward the people in front of them. "A familiar tale in my home as well. 'You're eight-and-twenty, Honoria. If you weren't a duke's daughter no gentleman would even give you the time of day'."

"Is eight-and-twenty really so old?"

She glanced up at the rather plaintive note in his voice, recalling too late that he was the same age. "It is for a woman. It's ancient for an unmarried woman."

"Then why haven't you married?"

An impertinent question if there ever was one. And one that she was not prepared to discuss in the middle of a grand ball.

"We were talking about you." She spied a set of open French windows ahead and inclined her head toward them. "Why don't we go out onto the terrace after all...that is, if there are no longer indecent acts being performed out there. I may have an idea that will help you, and we'll want a little privacy to talk."

He studied her face for a long moment, then nodded once and led her out into the night. The darkness was tempered by torches lit at regular intervals along the balustrade and a gibbous moon rising over the horizon.

Beside her Benedict breathed deeply in, exhaling with a gentle "Ah."

The cool air felt wonderful on Honoria's heated skin. But rather than say so she took the opportunity to tease him a little. "Too much for you in there?"

"I'd forgotten what a ballroom full of people *smelled* like. So many bodies crowded together, and every single one of them wearing some sort of fragrance. It's...oppressive. It pushes down upon one until the body can bear it no more."

They found a stone bench to one side and Honoria sat, arranging her skirts about her. "You miss Greece, don't you?"

He settled down next to her, his posture relaxing. "I do. But I didn't mean to be so vulgar about it. Please accept my apologies."

"There is no need to apologize to me for speaking frankly. You've said worse than that in my hearing, and I'm quite sure I have in yours. Or have you forgotten the time we 'liberated' that bottle of wine when we were fifteen?"

"I remember it well. You drank half of it before I could get through a glassful—"

"I did no such thing!"

"—and the next day you proceeded to describe to me in great detail just how very vile you felt."

He was laughing now, not a polite chuckle but a sound of genuine amusement. Honoria felt herself laughing along with him. "And you did the same. If memory serves, you even told me how many times you cast up your accounts."

His eyes rolled skyward. "Promise me you won't tell Lady Whitby that story. I would never hear the end of her etiquette lessons."

Honoria turned toward him, searching his face in the low light. "Has she been that meddlesome, then?"

Benedict shook his head, meeting her gaze as his mouth drew down into a more sober expression. "No. Well yes, she has, but I am trying not to mind—she simply has a vested interested in my future nuptials and wants to ensure they take place."

"Will you tell me about it?"

Honoria held her breath for a moment and waited. They used to tell each other everything, but when Benedict had put actual distance between them by sailing away to the Continent, an emotional distance had been created as well. It was one thing to share a fond memory, but what of the present?

His brows crowded together, the way they had when he'd thought intensely about something as a younger man. "She is the wife of a peer, and has given him no son to inherit. Nor likely will she."

"And so she's turned to matchmaking for you."

Her voice was soft and, when Benedict didn't respond, she thought perhaps he hadn't heard her. But then he nodded, bowing his head slightly. "She has."

"For her good, if not yours." Honoria grasped the stone bench with both her hands. "Well, I did say that I had an idea for you."

He straightened, his hair catching the torchlight—it had lightened considerably during his years away to a soft sandy brown. "I'm listening."

"You need to find a wife."

"Yes."

"But you can't dance."

His large hands clapped down over his knees. "What does one thing have to do with the other?"

Honoria put on the air of patient authority she used when conversing with her eight-year-old half-brother. "You must dance with a lady in order to court her. How else will you determine if you can even stand her company?"

"Can I not talk to her?"

Honoria shook her head, setting the ringlets on either side of her face to swaying. "Talking is not enough. One only discovers a person's true character when one speaks with that person alone. But when does a gentleman have the opportunity to speak alone with a lady?"

"We're alone now."

She looked for the twitching of his lips or crinkling of his eyes to suggest he was being facetious, but his serious expression remained fixed.

"We are. But how much longer will that last, do you think? How long before my stepmother begins to look for me?" Her fingers clenched the bench seat with more force. "And what would happen to my reputation if we were found together out here?"

"I see your point."

"Dancing accomplishes so much more. There is time for talking, of course, but there is also a chance to flirt, and to touch. One can study a partner's appearance without being rude or vulgar, and discover if said partner is graceful or clumsy or featherbrained or bookish."

Benedict sighed. "It's a necessity, then."

"Yes. And I will teach you."

"You?"

She tilted her head slightly to the side. "Me. Or you'll have to hire a dancing master."

She watched his fingers tense on his knees as he digested that bit of information. But he didn't reply.

A light breeze rustled the flowers in the garden nearby. The torch flames flickered, casting peculiar shadows across the terrace. Then all was still once more—including Benedict. She waited for several more minutes but he remained silent.

"Think it over, why don't you?" Honoria rose from the bench and smoothed the fine cambric of her gown. "Take me driving tomorrow, and we can discuss it further if you like."

Benedict stood and offered her his arm. "I'll call for you at four."

He fell quiet again escorting her back into the house, and she wondered if she'd offended him. No one liked to dwell on his own deficiencies, certainly. But the Benedict she knew six years ago would have teased her in return about a shortcoming of her own.

Clearly, he was no longer the man he'd once been.

"Honoria?"

She blinked herself out of her musings. "Yes?"

"I would marry you, you know."

She froze. "What?"

"If we were caught together. If I compromised you." His eyes met hers in the half-light. "And not just because I'm looking for a wife now. I would have then, too."

He didn't have to explain when *then* was. She knew he was thinking of the day her mother died. He never did tell her how he'd gained entry into the house or how he found her bedchamber without disturbing anyone, but he'd managed to do both late that night. He'd sat with her and held her hand as she had talked of her mother, then cradled her against him when she'd wept. Only when she had calmed did either of them realize the potential for an immense scandal his presence caused. And even then he'd stayed with her until she fell asleep.

Her fingers tightened on his sleeve in response. Perhaps some of the old Benedict still existed after all.

Chapter 2

BENEDICT GLANCED AT HONORIA OUT of the corner of his eye. She sat perfectly straight on the seat beside him with the skirt of her green dress arranged neatly about her. Her shoulders were relaxed, her hands were carefully folded around a reticule in her lap, and a small smile formed on her lips whenever she wasn't talking.

How did she do that?

They were driving in Whitby's curricle through Hyde Park—which is to say they were creeping slowly along in a throng of traffic, looking at other people and being looked at themselves. The driving itself was not a problem, nor even the barely discernible progress along Rotten Row. The sun shone down upon them and the air was still, allowing

Benedict to preserve a degree of masculinity and forgo wearing his greatcoat to keep warm. The horses, too, were agreeable: well-matched bays with a calm temperament, quite used to the hustle and bustle of the fashionable hour.

But personal scrutiny under any circumstances made him squirm. Here he felt like one of the Egyptian sculptures on display at the British Museum.

"Ah, Lord and Lady Tiverton. Good afternoon." Honoria discreetly tapped his arm three times, using a system they'd worked out beforehand to indicate the social importance of people they met. One tap was lowest among the *ton*; five taps meant prestige nearly on par with the Prince Regent himself.

Benedict gave a respectful nod to the couple in the slowly approaching barouche. "Lord Tiverton, Lady Tiverton."

"Lady Honoria, how does your father?" Lord Tiverton leaned toward the edge of his carriage, and his driver called the horses to a halt. "I have not seen him in Town yet."

Benedict tugged his own horses' reins as Honoria answered. "His Grace elected to remain in the country, my lord."

"Did he? For how long? I was hoping he would come with me to Tattersall's this month —no one knows horseflesh like the Duke of Alston."

Honoria's expression remained serene, but her body shifted slightly on the curricle seat. "I am not certain when he plans to return. But I will convey your wish when I write to him next."

Lord Tiverton frowned. "Perhaps I will write him myself as well."

She shifted again. "I am sure he would be pleased to hear from you."

They said their good-byes and resumed their tortoise-like pace. Honoria continued to acknowledge passersby with courteous nods, but Benedict noted that her smile was no longer the easy affectation it had been.

"Do you really not know when your father is coming to Town?" he asked in a quiet voice, the better to put off potential eavesdroppers. "It has been an age since I saw him last."

And there it was again—that slight movement of Honoria's person on the seat beside him, as if she were trying to ease an uncomfortable position without drawing attention to the action.

"No, I don't. He does not keep me apprised of all his plans."

"But I should think he would tell his only daughter when he would see her again."

"Well, he didn't." Honoria took a breath and let it out slowly. When she spoke again, her voice was bright with just a hint of scolding. "Why didn't you speak to Lord and Lady Tiverton? They don't have a daughter, but Lady Tiverton could certainly introduce to you any number of eligible ladies."

Benedict kept his eyes on the horses. "I didn't get a chance to speak to them. You and Lord Tiverton carried the whole conversation...all two minutes of it."

He felt her tap his arm twice and automatically looked to the curricle drawing near carrying two well dressed ladies. He nodded to the occupants, his mouth curving into what he hoped was a smile and not the grimace it felt like. The ladies acknowledged the greeting with genteel nods in return.

When the ladies had passed, Benedict addressed Honoria in a low tone. "How does your father, anyway? Has he taken one of his turns again? Is that why he's not in London?"

She paled but offered an artificial smile to a gentleman on horseback as he rode by. "Yes."

"Then why not say so to Lord Tiverton? His lordship knows about your father's delicate health—indeed, the whole of the *ton* knows."

Benedict turned to look at Honoria, *really* look at her. Her smile was still pasted on, but one hand clutched her reticule as if she feared someone would rip it from her, and her posture was rigid. Her eyes, too, refused to meet his. "Something has changed since last I was home."

"Not here." Her voice was nearly a whisper. She took another breath and continued with more authority. "There is a path a little way ahead. Turn down there—we'll be away from prying ears, but still properly within sight of the Row."

He returned his attention to the horses and did as instructed, ignoring oncoming conveyances despite Honoria's arm tapping. What use was small talk when a real problem was afoot?

When they were safely out of earshot, Benedict stopped the curricle and turned to Honoria.

"What has happened with your father?"

"What are you doing? We can't just sit here—everyone can see us!"

Benedict felt his brows draw together. "I thought that was the point."

"But we must appear as though everything is exactly as it should be. If we sit here in the middle of the path talking, all of society will know something is wrong."

"If we drive any further along this path, we'll be alone and out of sight. I didn't even bring a tiger on this outing—you'll be compromised."

She shook her head and gestured with one hand. "It loops around behind those trees, but comes out again over there. We can stop at the trees to talk and only be out of sight for a few moments."

That didn't sound exactly proper to Benedict, but what did he know about it? He'd been focused on stone statues for the last six years, not society gossips. He took up the reins and guided the horses to the place Honoria had indicated.

"Here?"

She nodded.

"Good. Will you tell me what's happened now?"

Her lips pressed together in a thin line and her gaze settled on a spot just to the left of his shoulder. But she didn't speak.

He reached for her hand and clasped it in his larger one, a gesture from their past he hoped she would remember. Words had always been easier for both of them to find when they were touching.

A smile flickered on her lips—recognition of their old form of reassurance or amusement because Benedict had forgotten to wear gloves? —before fading away. "Papa is ill again, yes. But it's different this time...worse. He can no longer walk the length of a room without stopping to catch his breath, and he's been coughing terribly. His physician says his heart is not beating normally, either, and that he complains of severe fatigue."

"Yet you came to London without him." It wasn't an accusation, but a statement of fact.

"He sent me away." Honoria's palm pressed against his, and he could feel the cold of her skin permeating her glove. "He is sure this is his end and wants to see me settled before he dies. I have the means to live independently, but Papa believes the world is a dangerous place for a female with no gentleman to protect her."

"And your brother is still a child. His Grace is right to worry." Benedict covered their clasped hands with his free one, trying to infuse some warmth into her chilly fingers. "You and I were once like family—you must know that I would always come to your aid should you need me."

"Certainly you would, if you were in the country."

He glanced down at their hands balanced on her knee and felt a twinge of regret. "I'm here now."

"But for how long? And what if something were to happen to you? Then I'd be right back where I am now, without even a widow's rights."

"So His Grace sent you here for the Season to find a husband."

He looked up just as her eyes darted to his. "Yes. But Benedict, who would I marry? This is my eleventh Season and I have yet to find a gentleman I could even spend an evening with, let alone a lifetime. Who could I trust enough to place all my worldly goods—and my very person—under his rule?"

"I could help you search." When she arched a dark eyebrow at him he drew back one hand. "I may not be familiar with the niceties of the *beau monde*, but I know a dishonorable man when I meet one."

"I'm sure you do." Her mouth curved into a wry smile, and her voice regained a note of her old self-assurance. "But I have a plan that will work for both of us."

"Of course you do." His mind conjured up images of Honoria's hastily concocted "plans" from their childhood and he felt the tension rising in his shoulders. But he plunged ahead. "Well then, let's hear it."

"I couldn't fall asleep last night, worrying over Papa," she told him, adjusting her hand in his clasp. For a brief moment she considered removing her own gloves and eliminating that barrier between them. But she dismissed the idea just as quickly—it wouldn't be seemly, and they were already pushing the boundaries of polite society by being out of sight. "So I tried distracting myself with your situation."

"A problem that may be solvable."

"Oh, it most certainly is. But you'll need more than just a dancing master, Benedict. There is dress to consider"—she squeezed his bare fingers—"and deportment. There are social customs to observe after you've met a lady who interests you, too. And I suspect you could use some practice in all of it."

His hazel eyes were steady, but his shoulders sagged a trifle. "No doubt I could."

"I could easily teach you. But what reason would we have for being so much together? The *ton* would wonder."

"We are old friends, Honoria. I don't think the *ton* would wonder too much at our association."

"They might wonder why you were spending so much time with me when you're supposed to be trying to find a wife."

His shoulders dropped a fraction more. "That is certainly possible."

"Which is why you shall pretend to court me."

"What?"

She rested her free hand on their clasped ones. "It's ideal, really. If you're courting me, it will be perfectly natural to call upon me at home, to dance with me at balls, to take me driving and on other outings. We can spend quite a lot of time together without meriting more than the usual notice."

"And you can write to His Grace to say you have a serious suitor."

"One who is more steadfast than the band of silly admirers I have now." Honoria patted their clasped hands. "He would be in transports of delight. You meet all of the practical criteria he has set out for me, and he's always liked you."

Benedict frowned, his sandy brows drawing together as he considered the idea. "But how will I look for a wife if I'm supposed to be interested in you?"

"Think of the courtship as a period of study," she said, knowing he would relate to an academic analogy. "I shall be your instructor in the ways of wooing a lady. When you have learned your lessons well, I'll cry off and you will be unattached."

"Cry off?"

"Didn't I mention the betrothal?" She flashed a grin at him, but then sobered. "I do think, for Papa's sake, we should announce a betrothal. A courtship is not binding, but a betrothal nearly is. I believe he will find it binding enough to content him."

Benedict lifted her loose hand from atop their clasped ones, and held both of hers in both of his. "I can see how a betrothal would ease your father's last days, but I cannot lie to him. And you know if he is to believe the engagement is real, I would need to speak with him in person."

"I am of age—I don't need his permission to marry."

"No, but there would be settlements to draw up. And His Grace would most certainly want to take care of the legalities before his time comes."

"Then what will we do?" She could hear the worry in her voice, try though she might to keep it steady. She needed Benedict's help much more than he needed hers, and she suspected he knew it.

He squeezed her hands and released them, turning to take up the reins. "We've been hidden behind these trees for far too long. And I need some time to think this over."

She faced the front of the curricle, smoothing down an invisible wrinkle in her skirt. "Of course. I've asked a lot of you today."

They drove the remainder of the path and rejoined the crowd, resuming their nodding and arm-tapping and mindless small talk. Benedict kept his expression impassive the whole while, and Honoria wished she knew what he was thinking. He was a man of honor and had been a good friend to both her and her father—which is why she had presented what she was beginning to think might be a foolish plan to him in the first place. But she knew that same sense of honor and friendship would resist deceiving her father, and that notion had kept her tossing and turning in the wee hours.

Because if Benedict refused to participate in her sham betrothal, Honoria would find herself shackled to a man who wanted her only for her bloodline or her dowry. For after eleven years on the Marriage Mart, the likelihood of finding love—going to the same entertainments with the same people she'd known all her adult life—was almost nonexistent.

And love was the only thing she wanted.

Honoria's maid brought a folded piece of paper to her as she sat embroidering with her aunt in the drawing room after dinner. She broke the plain seal and found the message within written in a clear, bold hand:

H,

I still have my doubts, but you asked for my help and I will give it. I will call tomorrow to discuss further details.

B

Honoria let out a sigh that was equal parts relief and affection. Her dear friend had come through for her.

Her aunt must have heard only the affection. "We'll have another gentleman caller tomorrow, then? One whom you'll actually welcome?"

Honoria smiled. "Yes. This one I will welcome very much."

Chapter 3

Honoria stood in the music room at Alston House a week later, taking stock of the items located there in preparation for Benedict's second visit of the afternoon. The days that had passed since his note had developed a kind of pattern: he would call in the afternoon with the gaggle of other gentlemen hopeful of winning Honoria's hand, then he'd return later to take her driving in the park. He didn't seem to enjoy either activity, so she had tried to impress upon him the need to not only express his attentiveness to her, but to make sure the others noticed it as well. Sympathy would run high for a gentleman who had been thrown over by his lady after demonstrating nothing but thoughtfulness and loyalty to her.

But in an entire week, he never managed to stay in her drawing room for more than twenty minutes. It was probably the topics of conversation, she decided. Her other callers spoke of who was wearing what at which soirée the previous night, the highlights of the latest Minerva Press novel, the beauty of the flowers they sent compared to her own—things they thought she would find interesting. But apparently they bored Benedict beyond reason.

He did show some progress during their Hyde Park outings, though. He'd become adept at asking a question about a subject near and dear to his conversational partner's heart, and listening attentively to the reply. For the brief interviews during the fashionable hour, it was a beautiful strategy—especially with Honoria murmuring ideas to him as they drove. With just a few words he appeared courteous and personable. And, if he was truly paying attention to the answers he received, he was learning quite a lot about the people that moved in society.

Today was going to be quite a different challenge, though. Honoria directed two footmen to move aside this piece of furniture or that, to roll up the carpets and carefully place them against a wall. She shuffled through the music she had laid out on the pianoforte, set it down, then picked it all up again, wondering if any of the pieces would do after all.

Today was to be Benedict's first dancing lesson.

"Mr. Grey has arrived—I told Engle to show him here rather than the drawing room."

Honoria turned to see her aunt gliding through the music room door wearing a bright smile and her best yellow day dress.

Honoria returned the smile and smoothed down her own floral print. Against Benedict's objection, Aunt Cecilia had been told about Honoria's plan—or, at least, the part about Benedict needing dancing lessons. She was residing with Honoria for the duration of the Season, so there was no way to have him in the house for any useful length of time without Aunt Cecilia discovering him. Nor would she have reacted well had anyone questioned her at a *ton* event about his comings and goings.

And somebody had to provide the music.

"Good. I was half afraid he would disappear into another excavation."

Aunt Cecilia snorted. "Not if he's anything like his father was at that age. Lord George Grey would take on any challenge—the more difficult it was, the more effort he'd put into it. And for some men, dancing is more than a little difficult."

"Was Lord George a good dancer?"

"I should say so. He cut quite the dashing figure, too—young ladies were setting their caps for him before they even came out."

Honoria raised an eyebrow inquisitively. "Including you, Aunt?"

"Oh yes," Aunt Cecilia answered without hesitation. "Not only was he handsome, but kind too. Your Mr. Grey is bookish like his mother, but he has his father's kindness."

Honoria was drifting toward one of the large windows that faced out onto the square, but paused to glance back at her aunt. "Do you think so?"

Aunt Cecilia nodded, heading toward the pianoforte and making herself comfortable on the bench. "Did you not see him at the Lambert ball last night? Lucy Drake was sitting all alone during the supper dance—she's nearly as old as you, and her only dowry is those awful smallpox scars on her face. Well, your Mr. Grey went over and sat with her through the rest of the set, and was very attentive to her at supper too. They didn't seem to talk much, but I doubt Lucy minded."

Honoria turned her face toward the sun shining into the room and felt herself smiling. "I did not know, but I'm not surprised. He is very kind indeed. But," she continued, turning away from the window, "you must stop call him *my* Mr. Grey. He isn't—"

A masculine voice interrupted Honoria's protest. "He is. For the next hour or so, at any rate."

Benedict stood just inside the door, and Honoria took the opportunity to look him over. He wore a charcoal cutaway coat over a gray-blue waistcoat and buckskin breeches. His shirt and cravat were crisp and white, his tall black Hessians polished to a high shine. Every stitch on him was unadorned, even plain. But the fabrics were fine and the tailoring equally so.

They suited him remarkably well.

"Your valet seems to have taken our conversation to heart."

Benedict gave her a little bow. "I don't know how he put up with me all those years in Greece. But he's like a new man since you've deemed my appearance to be important."

Honoria felt the corners of her mouth curving upward again. "You look a bit changed yourself—you're standing a little taller I think."

"It's probably my coat. The style is a bit tighter now than I remember. It rather forces one to stand straight with shoulders back." He came the rest of the way into the room and greeted Aunt Cecilia, then settled himself on the largest sofa to pull off his boots—with more struggle than he probably would have liked— and exchange them for the dancing pumps he carried. "There now. If I step on your toes, there's a chance I won't smash them completely."

"You used to be a fair dancer," Honoria reminded him, leading him to the space the footmen had cleared.

"I used to be a passable dancer," he corrected as she turned to face him.

"Then we shall begin with something easy. Aunt, the Beethoven minuet please."

"A minuet? Isn't that rather old fashioned?"

"Yes, but the time signature and tempo are right."

"For what?"

She noticed a woodsy, slightly sweet fragrance as he stopped an arm's length from her. It reminded her of the apple orchard at her father's country seat, where she and Benedict used to read when the weather was fine.

"A waltz."

He took a step back and the scent faded. "Honoria, no woman with any sense of propriety dances the waltz. Even I know that."

"Some do, actually. It's becoming more accepted now." She held out a hand to him. "Besides, there's very little memorizing involved in a waltz. It's more about rhythm than specific figures, so I thought it would be a good place to start your re-education."

He didn't respond, and she briefly wondered if he practiced doing so. Not reacting at all often seemed to be his reply these days.

Or did he simply think things over more carefully now?

She wiggled the fingers of her outstretched hand. "You never have to dance it in public if it feels too unseemly to you."

That got a smile out of him, and came forward once more to take her hand. "Very well. You are the dancing mistress today."

The applewood fragrance returned and she realized that Benedict was its source. Interesting considering his condemnation of wearing scent at Lady Whitby's Black and White Ball. She took hold of his other hand and felt....*something*. It was the first time he'd touched her since their talk in the park, and both their hands were bare this time. Was that why it felt different? Or was it something else?

"It's a one-two-three, one-two-three rhythm like the minuet—and you just step." She guided him by the hands slowly around the empty space, counting aloud. "That's right, one big step, two little ones. One, two, three. One, two, three..."

"I feel ridiculous."

But he didn't stop, and so she gave him what she hoped was an encouraging smile. "That's because there's no music."

"Maybe there should be."

"All right, then music you shall have. Whenever you're ready, Aunt Cecilia. Slowly, please." Honoria halted and gave his hands a little squeeze. How warm and strong they were. "Just listen for a few measures and get a feel for it. When you're ready, step off and I'll follow you."

He nodded, his brows drawn together. In concentration or uncertainty?

Both, she decided a few moments later. The song was halfway over before Benedict made a move, and Honoria could see him mouthing "one-two-three" as he stepped with her around the center of the room, his gaze cemented to his feet. When the last note died away, his eyes met hers.

"How was that?"

"Not bad for your first try. Let's do it again."

His nod was matter-of-fact, but his lips curved into a smile that said he was clearly pleased. Honoria signaled and Aunt Cecilia played the piece again, just as slowly as before. But Benedict was ready, and he began his steps only a few measures in this time. He held Honoria's hands firmly and his movements were careful. But each time they repeated the song, Honoria saw his shoulders relax a fraction more and his eyes lift a little from the floor.

"I don't know what all the fuss is about," he said as the last note grew fainter. "There's nothing scandalous about this."

"We aren't to the scandalous part yet. Should we do that next?"

Benedict was rather proud of himself—he was taking to dancing with more ease than he ever imagined he would. Not that he was a particularly clumsy man, but neither had he ever been particularly graceful. He could even imagine himself waltzing with a lady in front of an assemblage of aristocrats without fear of disgracing himself.

Then Honoria dashed his imagined scene to tiny pieces.

His eyes widened as she drew him closer and placed his right hand on the small of her back. When she reached her left hand up to his shoulder, his body went rigid—these liberties were permitted at balls and assemblies in front of other people?

"Relax." She said the word softly, almost under her breath.

He wasn't sure if she was speaking to him or herself, but decided that the idea was a good one in either case. He tightened the muscles in his shoulders and held them so for a moment, then let go. Some of the tension remained, but some of it bled away and he felt his shoulders loosen.

She turned his free hand palm-up and placed hers in it. "There are other positions in which to waltz, but this is the one I like best. It feels the most natural."

"It's like an embrace. You've really danced like this with other gentlemen?"

She tilted her head back and laughed a little. "Yes, though not too many times. And— fortunately—never with someone I wasn't fond of. Are you ready?"

He adjusted his hand on her back, fitting it snugly against the curve of her body. "I think so."

"Step off with your right foot, just like before, and use your hands to turn me. Think of this"—she squeezed his left hand—"as the prow of a ship. You lead with that. This"—her other hand slid down his arm —"is like a rudder. A little pressure one way or the other on my back, and I'll know which way to turn."

He nodded. He could do this, if he could just concentrate on the steps rather than the woman so unexpectedly close to him. "Got it."

She replaced her hand on his shoulder. "We're ready, Aunt."

The music began and Benedict stood still for a few moments, trying to get a feeling for the mechanics of the steps in this new position. Honoria's expression and body were relaxed as she waited in the half-circle of his arm, as if she was perfectly comfortable being there.

That contentment flowed from her limbs into his and he stepped off into the dance, pulling Honoria with him...and nearly tumbled the pair of them to the ground.

The music stopped abruptly and Benedict held tight to his partner trying to regain his balance. "That was not the start I had hoped for."

"No, I suppose not. Let's try again." Her mouth was near his ear, and he heard her amusement rather than saw it.

Once they righted themselves, they did try again. And again. Each time they made it a little deeper into the music without mishap, but Benedict still couldn't shake the intimacy of what they were doing. Honoria's hand had slipped from his shoulder to take hold of his upper arm, possibly because he was six or seven inches taller than she was—he was sure that her hand on his shoulder was an uncomfortable reach for prolonged periods. Or perhaps she had a more secure hold on his arm than on his shoulder. However unintentionally, he'd tossed her about the room a good deal today.

But it felt like more than that...or at the very least, like it *could* be more.

That thought unsettled him. He and Honoria had been friends for nearly twenty years, and he'd never thought of her in any other way. But this sudden search for a wife coupled with the close contact of the waltz set his mind working. On the surface, a union between them would be brilliant. They were of similar rank and fortune—or would be when he inherited—and one of the properties entailed to Benedict's future marquessate adjoined one held by Honoria's father. There would also no longer be a reason to lie to His Grace, which would lighten Benedict's heart considerably. Honoria would make a fine marchioness, too, when the time came. That they were at ease in each other's company only sweetened the deal.

Was that enough, though? Others had married for less, certainly. Benedict had been considering such a marriage himself—was still considering it. But how would Honoria feel about such an arrangement?

"Ready?"

Her voice brought him back to the task at hand. "Yes. Perhaps we'll make it through the entire song this time."

The music started and Benedict focused on getting his feet to go where they were supposed to. One-two-three, one-two-three, one-two-three...

"Your dress keeps brushing against my legs." The words were out of his mouth before he'd even finished thinking them, and he felt heat rising in his cheeks. Why did he have to mention that?

Honoria only grinned. "Just be thankful I'm not wearing one of those huge gowns from the previous generation. Some of them were so wide a lady had to turn sideways to fit through the door."

"That could not have been terribly comfortable." One-two-three, one-two-three...so far, no stumbles...

"No. Nor was it terribly flattering. I can't think of a woman alive who could wear one of those monstrosities and look well in it."

One-two-three, one-two-three... "You could."

"Oh, I doubt it." Honoria had never been one to fish for compliments, and the tone of her voice said she wasn't doing so now. The laughter in her dark eyes agreed. "I'd be wider than I am tall!"

He smiled. "And you'd still be pretty. You always have been."

Once again the words were out of his mouth before they'd fully formed in his mind, but he wasn't embarrassed by them this time. A little confused, perhaps, as "pretty" began to take on a new connotation after his unexpected thoughts of marriage with Honoria. But not embarrassed. He'd only spoken the truth, after all.

And had apparently surprised her with it—her brows had risen for a moment before she replied, "You've never told me that before."

He tugged her into a turn to avoid a side table they'd danced too close to. "I should have done. Not that you didn't hear it often enough from others, but you should hear it from those you're closest to once in a while as well. I'll try not to wait twenty years to say it again."

The last note from the pianoforte echoed through the partially cleared room and Benedict released his partner, bowing low before her. She executed a grand curtsy in return, then clapped her hands.

"We did it! Not a single misstep through the whole piece."

She'd said "we" not "you", and for some reason that pleased him enormously. "We did. Perhaps there's hope for me after all."

He declined tea when it was offered and said his farewells, rather anxious now to be home where he could think in peace. Because he had a great deal more to think about now than when he'd risen that morning.

Chapter 4

"**I**'M GIVEN TO UNDERSTAND YOU'VE chosen a wife."

"What?"

Whitby entered Benedict's library, as was his custom, close on the heels of the butler. "You've been paying a lot of attention to one lady," he said, striding across the room and dropping into a wing chair opposite his cousin. "That sets tongues a-wagging."

"You mean Honoria? We have been friends for a long time—you know that."

"Friends who suddenly go driving every day, after the gentleman has called at the lady's home."

Benedict glanced at the book in his hands, then hunted around for a place marker. His cousin was sometimes a little too plain-spoken, but he was also clever and often gave good advice—which Benedict could sorely use. He found the marker and placed the book carefully on the table beside him. "Is there gossip?"

"People have noticed."

"Including your lady wife."

Whitby nodded. "She approves, by the way. She says Lady Honoria would be good for you, balance you out a bit."

"Balance me out?"

Whitby leaned back and chuckled. "You know how academic you can be, how quiet. If it were up to you, you'd spend all your time in here. But the lady has you out of the house. And I daresay you've been more social at entertainments since you started courting her —Lady Whitby says you hold actual conversations with people now."

That was the plan, of course, though Whitby didn't know it. Good to hear it was working.

"I still don't enjoy it. Since socializing is a necessity for finding a wife, I've been making the attempt."

Whitby smiled broadly. "It seems to have worked."

Benedict must have scowled, or at least frowned, because his cousin sat up a little straighter in his chair.

"You do have honorable intentions toward the lady, don't you?"

"I'm not exactly a rakehell, now, am I? And I would never do anything to hurt Honoria." Did Benedict sound as defensive to Whitby as he did to himself?

"Something else is troubling you then. What is it?"

Benedict hesitated, his mind groping for the right words. "How did you know Lady Whitby was the right woman for you?"

"Ah." Whitby relaxed back against the soft upholstery of his wing chair. "It's like that, is it?"

"Like what?"

"You want to marry for love."

And Benedict realized he did. Thoughts of his father crept into his mind, giving a young Benedict facetious advice about how to deal with females. *When she sets her mouth in a firm line like that, son, you'd best do whatever she wants,* Lord George Grey would say while grinning at his lady wife. Or, *One thing you learn when you become a husband is to say the words "yes my love" without even hearing the question. Because the answer is always yes.* But for all his teasing, Benedict's father did impart one important lesson to his son: a good husband loves his wife with all his heart. He never said it aloud, but he never had to; though it wasn't fashionable to be too fond of one's spouse, anyone with eyes could see how deeply Lord George had cared for his bride.

Did Benedict love Honoria like that? If he had to think about it, probably not.

But *could* he?

Whitby was nodding. "It's a tradition in our family, you know. Great-grandfather Whitby was supposed to marry a lady his father had chosen, but he fell in love with another and married her instead."

"And he encouraged his children to follow their hearts, too. I remember that story." Benedict felt his brows crowd together. "It turned out well for him. But what if you don't know what your heart wants?"

"Then you'll just have to wait until it tells you."

"That's not very helpful."

Whitby laughed. "A little too poetic for you, is it? How about this, then. Take note of how you feel when you spend time with her. Then note how you feel when you're not with her. If you'd rather be with her more often than not, your heart is starting to speak up."

"And what if I find I do love her, but she doesn't love me?"

"That, my friend, is when the poetry will start to make sense."

Benedict had been drawn to Lord Elgin's venture in Athens not only because it meant cataloging and preserving the remains of an ancient culture, but also because—if one observed carefully—those remains could tell a person an enormous amount about that culture. It was like putting clues together to solve a mystery, divining what a long-dead civilization might have been like.

Now he decided to turn his skill as an anthropologist on his situation with Honoria.

He was escorting her with her aunt to a concert given by the new Philharmonic Society at the Argyll Rooms, and decided this would be the perfect opportunity to begin a full-scale scientific study. He would take Whitby's suggestion and observe how he felt about Honoria throughout the evening. Taking the inquiry a step further, he also resolved to study *her* reactions to *him* during their time together. Perhaps he could learn not only of his own heart's desire, but something of hers as well.

She was presently engaged in conversation with a gentleman who looked too young to have even begun shaving. Tall and slender, he had curly blond hair that rebelled against the pomade with which he'd attempted to slick it back, and a ready smile for Honoria's every comment. She was gazing up at him, eyes a little wide, both hands gripping the fan she carried, as if he was the most fascinating man in London.

"Have you met Lord Thomas?" Honoria's aunt appeared beside Benedict, nodding in the direction of her niece.

"I haven't had the pleasure."

"Neither have I, but I knew his mother. Shall we go and speak to them? Honoria can introduce us."

Benedict thought he heard a note of mischief in her voice to go with the grin she'd flashed him. Her face, however, held nothing but polite inquiry only a moment later.

He offered her his arm and tried to approach the pair with the eyes of a scientist. Honoria's posture was straight as an arrow, her head tilted back to look this Lord Thomas in the eyes. As Benedict came closer, though, he could see her gaze drop to her companion's shoulder before returning to his face. Her thumb, too, absently strummed a rib of her fan.

"Honoria, dear, who is this handsome gentleman that has so captured your attention this evening?"

Honoria turned toward her aunt's voice and smiled—the same smile she used during her drives with Benedict. "This is Lord Thomas Morgan, son of the Duke of Whittington. Lord Thomas, my aunt Lady Cecilia Maitland, and Mr. Benedict Grey."

Lord Thomas reached for Lady Cecilia's hand, bowing so low over it he nearly brushed his lips across her knuckles. "I see now from which side of the family Lady Honoria's beauty originates."

Lady Cecilia smiled indulgently. "I was not aware you possessed such a silver tongue, Lord Thomas...nor such a keen eye with it."

Benedict fought to keep his eyes from rolling. The ladies and Lord Thomas, however, laughed politely at the little joke.

"Lord Thomas was just telling me about his reading preferences," Honoria said, changing the subject with a glance in Benedict's direction. "Shakespeare, was it not?"

Lord Thomas released Lady Cecilia's hand and flicked his gaze toward Benedict, too, before returning his attention to Honoria. "Yes, my lady. Only this afternoon I was reading *Romeo and Juliet* and thought of you:

But, soft! what light through yonder
window breaks?
It is the east, and Juliet is the sun.
Arise, fair sun, and kill the envious moon,
Who is already sick and pale with grief,
That thou her maid art far more fair than
she."

Benedict bit down on the inside of his cheek, just hard enough to keep himself from making a comment, but Honoria seemed pleased. Or was that another version of her society smile?

"Well done, my lord. I would hear more, but I believe it's time we took our seats."

"Allow me to escort you."

Lord Thomas offered his arm to Honoria and strode off with her, which left Benedict trailing behind with Honoria's aunt.

"I wouldn't worry, Mr. Grey." Lady Cecilia laid her hand on Benedict's offered arm as they walked. "The boy has no serious interest in my niece."

"How do you know that?"

"Did you see the way he looked at you before quoting Shakespeare? Lord Thomas is barely two-and-twenty, and a third son with no income other than the allowance he receives from his father. He knows he can't compete with you—probably why he chose such an overused passage. Nor did it seem as if Honoria wanted him to try."

"I thought she looked a trifle bored."

"I suspect she was," Lady Cecilia agreed. "Perhaps she was wondering if *someone* was planning a visit to her father."

Already? "It has only been two weeks, my lady."

"Two weeks in which you've been to the house nearly every day, Mr. Grey. And it's not as though the pair of you were strangers before now."

"No," Benedict replied slowly. He doubted Honoria would have asked him for a pretend courtship if they had been newly acquainted. "But we have been apart for some time."

"That is true. Perhaps, if you aren't otherwise engaged after the concert, you'd be agreeable to a little refreshment at Alston House?" Lady Cecilia winked at him. "It will easier to become reacquainted without a crowd of gentlemen vying for her attention, will it not?"

Benedict allowed himself a smile. Honoria's aunt had been away for much of the time he'd spent with her family when he was growing up, so he hadn't known her all that well. But she'd always been slightly scandalous, and he was grateful for it now. Inviting a single gentleman to your home at night wasn't exactly the done thing, even if Benedict would never be alone with either lady. But he could definitely make use of some real conversational time with Honoria.

"It is certainly easier to speak with a lady when one is not trying desperately not to step on her toes."

Lady Cecilia chuckled. "I daresay you're right about that."

Between listening to the music and socializing at the interval meaningful dialogue during the concert turned out to be nonexistent. So Benedict was doubly grateful when he was seated beside Honoria on a cornflower blue sofa in the drawing room at Alston House later that evening. Lady Cecilia situated herself with a glass of brandy and her sewing basket near enough to the couple to talk to them without shouting, but far enough away that they could speak to each other with a degree of privacy.

Benedict mentally applauded her cleverness.

"Did you enjoy the concert this evening?"

"I did," Honoria answered, her voice full of enthusiasm and pitched just right for her aunt to hear. "The full power of the orchestra when they played the symphony just before the interval...it just isn't something you get from a pianoforte in your home, is it?" When he smiled briefly but gave no verbal response, she discreetly touched the back of his hand. "Did you enjoy the concert?"

Her skin was warm upon his. "I don't know much about music, but I do like to listen to it. And the Society was especially good. The Greek and Roman references were a nice touch, too."

"'Numa Pompilius' and 'Anacreon'? I thought you might find that aspect appealing."

"What about the Renaissance reference? Lord Thomas and his Shakespeare—did you find that appealing?" He said it with a teasing tone, and she laughed.

"Why Mr. Grey, are you jealous?"

"Should I be?" He turned his hand over beneath hers and lowered his voice. "We are supposed to be courting, after all."

She slid slightly closer to him. "He's harmless...merely practicing on me what he hopes will win another. Like you are."

"You must be an exceptional teacher to have two pupils engaging your services."

"Ah, but I was merely a brief test for Lord Thomas, not his teacher." She curled her fingers around his. "You are my only pupil."

He bent his head toward hers and caught the hint of a scent that was both familiar and unknown at the same time. It reminded him of spring and sunshine and books, but he couldn't quite identify it.

"Lucky for me." He closed his hand around hers—it felt good to hold. "And lucky for you. I need as much help as you can give me, I'm afraid."

Her eyes dropped to the cushion where their clasped hands lay. "I didn't think you knew the word 'afraid'."

He gave a short laugh. "Me? Truly?"

"How many times did you board a ship and travel round a continent? How long did you spend in a country where the weather and food and language are so different?"

"You think I wasn't afraid?" he asked softly, giving her hand a gentle squeeze. "I was terrified every moment of every sea voyage. The entire time I was in Athens I lived in fear that something ancient and priceless that I was supposed to protect would be smashed to bits, or that the constant armed conflict in Serbia was going to spill over into Greece."

"But you went anyway. Even after you'd come home to England the first time, you went back."

"The reward was well worth the risk."

Her dark eyes—the same color as the chocolate he'd discovered she liked to drink every morning—lifted to meet his. "You are a brave man, Benedict Grey. Your future wife will either be immensely proud of you, or extremely frightened for your safety."

"Which would you be?"

Her brows lifted in surprise for a moment, before dropping down as she considered her answer. "Both, I expect. Especially when you were off somewhere excavating some other historical site."

"You wouldn't come with me?"

She tilted her head slightly to the side. "I might. It would calm my mind to see you with my own eyes each day. But I would miss the Season tremendously. I like to dance, to gossip, to flirt—"

"I noticed."

Her smile returned and she swatted his arm with her free hand. "What would you know of flirting? I have yet to see you do it once."

"I may not know how to do it, but I certainly recognize it when I see it. Besides, it's you I'm supposed to be smitten with." He caught Honoria's hand as it retreated and kissed it quickly.

Lady Cecilia's gaze flickered up from her sewing, but she said nothing. It was enough, though, to remind Benedict that there was another person in the room.

"Perhaps it's time I take my leave." He planted a swift kiss on Honoria's other hand and released them both. "Aren't we working on country dances tomorrow?"

"We are," she confirmed, her smile growing.

"Then I'll need to rest well tonight." Benedict rose from the sofa and bowed to Lady Cecilia, who acknowledged him with a nod.

Honoria stood with him and lit a candle from the brace burning nearby. "I'll see you out."

She slipped her arm through his as they maneuvered through the house down to the ground level. A sleepy footman came forward with Benedict's hat and gloves as they reached the front door, then melted away into the dark.

Honoria set the candle on a table near the front door and turned to face Benedict. "I can't remember when I've had a more delightful evening."

"I'm not sure that I can, either."

The light from the candle was just bright enough to illuminate her face and he found himself overwhelmed by the desire to touch her one more time. He brushed his fingers over the soft skin of her cheek, then bent forward to allow his lips to follow. When he attempted to draw back, he felt her arms slide around his shoulders and hold him in place. She raised herself up on her toes and pressed her lips against his.

If there was any rational thought left in his brain, it exited right then.

His arms came around her, pulling her snugly against his body as his mouth opened over hers. He was gratified when she followed suit and kissed him back, a bit clumsily but oh so sweetly—once, twice more before lowering herself down.

"Good night, Benedict," she said. Her voice sounded as dazed as he felt.

"Good night," he managed in return.

How he got through the door and down the steps, he didn't know, but he found himself on the pavement, hat and gloves in hand, wondering what to do. Lady Cecilia had insisted they use the Alston carriage for the concert, so the ladies had come to his house in St. James Square before proceeding to the Argyll Rooms. He could probably find a hackney somewhere nearby, but decided walking at least part of the way would do him some good. As usual, he needed to think. Had he the answer to the question of his feelings for Honoria, or hers for him? Or was it simply a physical attraction that had sprung up between the two of them?

Either way, perhaps he should consider more seriously that visit to the duke.

Chapter 5

Honoria fairly bounced out of bed the next morning, despite the long hours she'd lain awake during the night.

She'd kissed Benedict!

She still wasn't clear on what had possessed her to do such a thing, nor was she terribly sure what his response would be in the cold light of day. But at the moment she didn't care. He had held her as if nothing was more dear to him in the world, and she'd felt so safe in his arms.

She hadn't realized how much she'd needed that safety, that strength, until last night.

"There's a note here from Mr. Grey," her maid said, bustling into the room with a tray. "I thought you might want to read it while you had your chocolate this morning."

"Oh yes, thank you." Honoria poured herself a cup and broke the seal on the letter—he'd used his own this time rather than leaving it plain. She scanned the page quickly trying to get an overall sense of what he'd written, then went back and read again at a pace more conducive to comprehension.

"He's asked me to visit Whitby House with him this afternoon, to take tea with his mother and the marchioness."

"That's exciting," the maid replied with a bright smile.

"Or completely terrifying. I've met them both before, of course, but not..."

The maid nodded. Not as a prospective member of the family. For that is how they would see her, as Benedict's potential bride. Was that how he saw her now, too? Did he feel obligated to marry her after their kiss last night, even though no one knew about it but the two of them?

Or was this just the next logical step in their ruse? It certainly made sense—if Benedict had truly been courting her, an invitation from the female members of his family would be expected. But it was not something Honoria had prepared herself for. She would have to go into their home and essentially lie to them about her future with their cousin and son.

Exactly as Benedict would do with her father.

Well, there was nothing for it—just because she had been blind to its coming didn't mean she could avoid this complication. Especially not when her partner in this business was prepared to do much the same for her. She called for a pen and some paper and dashed off a reply to Benedict informing him that she would be ready at the appointed time.

But what to wear? She and her maid combed through the gowns in her dressing room, considering this one or that one, rejecting others out of hand. Together they pulled out several gowns for Honoria to try, and spread them out across her bed. Each time her maid got her laced in to one, Honoria would stand in front of the cheval glass turning slowly left and right before shaking her head.

She finally settled on a blush-colored muslin sprigged with tiny roses. Ordered last month, she had yet to wear it anywhere so it could serve as a topic of conversation if need be. The color was beautifully feminine and Honoria knew she looked well in it, which gave her confidence a much-needed lift.

She was ready by the time he arrived and elected not to make him wait, though her aunt suggested that spending a few minutes alone in the drawing room wouldn't go amiss with a gentleman. Honoria simply smiled and hurried down the main staircase.

His greeting to her was very correct, his face expressionless, as though he didn't remember that only twelve hours earlier they had been in each other's arms on this very spot. Nor did he reveal any emotion as he helped her into a carriage with the Whitby crest emblazoned on it.

When he settled himself on the seat across from her and not next to her, she decided she'd had enough. She stood carefully, one hand on the ceiling of the carriage for balance, and turned herself onto the plush velvet beside Benedict.

"Honoria, what are you doing?"

"You were pressed against me from shoulders to knees last night, but you can't sit beside me?

He blushed—a full, flaming blush, his cheeks and ears flooded with red. "I can't seem to think when you're close to me."

"That's what every lady wants to hear, that she turns gentlemen to blathering idiots," she replied, crossing her arms.

Benedict leaned forward, resting his forearms on his thighs. "That's not what I meant. I just—the nearer you are to me, the more I think about that embrace. And I need all my wits about me for this visit. We both do."

That he couldn't stop thinking about the two of them together wasn't necessarily a good thing. Was he obsessing about a lack of good judgment? Was he regretting a moment of weakness?

Was he, perhaps, a little bit in love with her?

She relaxed her arms and let her hands fall loosely into her lap. "We need to talk about last night."

He acknowledged her statement with a slow nod. "We do. But that is not a conversation to be rushed—we'll need more time than this drive will give us. Am I still invited for dancing lessons later?"

"Yes, of course. Though I'm not sure what we'll work on. The cotillion is for four couples, which we don't have, and I don't think you're quite ready for a Scotch reel yet."

That drew a small smile from him, though only his mouth was involved in the action. "You're probably right about that. Do you think your aunt would object if we walked in the garden instead? We could talk then."

"Short of leaving us alone in a room with the door closed, Aunt Cecilia is rather amenable to whatever we'd like. I think she'll not object to a walk in the garden."

"Good." He reached for one of her hands and gave it the briefest of squeezes.

Then he moved himself to the seat across from her and rode the rest of the way in silence.

Upon arriving at Whitby House in Park Lane they were whisked directly upstairs to the drawing room. Benedict resumed his powers of speech long enough to introduce Honoria to his mother, Lady George Grey, and his cousin's wife.

"Yes dear, we know Lady Honoria," his mother laughed as she resumed her seat. "There's no need to be quite so formal."

Thank goodness for that. This visit was going to be awkward enough without throwing in uncomfortable formalities.

"Come sit here," Lady George said, indicating a settee near her own chair, "and we'll have a nice, comfortable coze."

Honoria did as she was bid, both relieved and uneasy when Benedict made to sit beside her.

"Oh no, Benedict," Lady Whitby interrupted when he was midway between standing and sitting, "Whitby asked that I send you to him in his study. Something about carriages or curricles or something."

"Oh, yes." He straightened quickly, his ears turning faintly red.

"Are you ordering a new carriage at last?" Lady George asked, clasping her hands together in her lap.

Benedict cleared his throat. "A phaeton, perhaps. A town carriage at a later date." His eyes roamed down to Honoria. "I can't continually borrow conveyances from Whitby whenever we wish to go somewhere."

He was either masterfully selling their imminent faux betrothal, or he was nervous and looking to her to steady himself. Oddly, she was pleased with either motive.

When Benedict had shut the door behind him, Lady Whitby poured tea and began her genteel interrogation.

"Does he often follow you around like that?"

Honoria found she was a little insulted by the question on Benedict's behalf—it made him sound like a lost little puppy. The man had some difficulties in ballrooms and drawing rooms to be sure, but he'd taken over the running of an operation that brought several shiploads of invaluable historic cargo to England. How many others could say that?

"He's a bit protective, I think," she replied, lifting her teacup to her mouth for a sip. Not a lie—he'd always been protective of Honoria—though she'd been doing her share of protecting, too, these past weeks, if in a more subtle fashion.

"That's Benedict," Lady George added with a warm smile. "Do you remember him after his father died? Though he was but a boy, he escorted me everywhere I went—even if it was only from one side of the house to another."

The memory came back to Honoria in images. She and Benedict had been, what? Ten? Eleven? She remembered digging in the gardens not far from one of the old marquess's country houses, looking for medieval battlefields and ancient settlements. And lounging on the terrace when the weather was hot, conjugating Latin verbs together. All this time she thought Lady George had asked Benedict to stay close, when in reality he'd been keeping watch over his mother.

"He's always been mindful of those he cares for," Lady Whitby said, her eyes flickering toward Honoria. "What's your opinion of this phaeton he's purchasing?"

"I was not aware until today that he was considering it." Honoria resisted the urge to shrug. "Benedict is entitled to purchase whatever he likes."

"I heard he was also thinking of refurbishing his house in St. James Square," the marchioness continued with well-practiced casualness. "Or perhaps even beginning a search for a larger home."

"Now that's just gossip," Lady George cautioned.

"But it would be noteworthy if it were true."

Both women were looking at Honoria now, Lady Whitby with stark interest and Lady George with what appeared to be hope.

Drat them.

And drat Honoria's thoughtless plan.

She sipped her tea again. "How nice for him."

Lady George blinked, seeming to realize that she'd been staring. "Honoria, might I ask you some questions of a more...personal nature?"

Oh dear. "You may."

"Do you care for my son?"

"Yes, of course," Honoria responded without hesitation. That she could answer truthfully lessened some of the weight on her conscience.

"And do you want to see him happy?"

"I always have." Another truth, another measure of weight lifted.

Lady George paused, fiddling with her teacup before asking the next question. "Do you think you can make him happy?"

Honoria carefully set her own teacup in its saucer. She knew what she was supposed to say, that she would do everything in her power to keep Benedict happy for as long as they were wed. And if they had actually planned to marry, she likely would have said such a thing. But they never had such plans, and Honoria found she could not lie to his mother after all.

"I-I don't know. I can only hope the decisions we make are the right ones...for both of us." Honoria realized her answer didn't quite match the question, but knew it was the best she could do.

Lady George smiled once more, a little wistfully. "It was brave of you to answer so honestly. But then, you've always been a brave girl. Especially these last few years, else you would not have waited all this time for Benedict to return home."

Double drat—she thought Honoria had remained unmarried in hopes that Benedict would propose, as if they had fallen in love early on and were parted by circumstance.

That was one myth she could not perpetuate. "You make is sound as if we came to some sort of arrangement before he went to Athens. But Lady George, we never did—it wasn't like that between us."

"Perhaps not," the lady said, undaunted. "But I've seen the way he looks at you, and the way you look at him. Your minds may not have settled anything between you, but your hearts have done so some time ago."

Honoria shook her head gently. Her heart had nothing to do with this, even if her body had begun to put forth its own ideas. "I don't think so."

But Lady George would not be dissuaded— another thing Honoria would have to discuss with Benedict when he came to Alston House.

If she ever made it there herself. This visit was beginning to feel as though it would never end.

"Thank heavens you're here, Mr. Grey," Lady Cecilia said as she rushed down the main staircase.

Benedict's head snapped up, the gloves he'd been removing forgotten in an instant at the worry that laced her voice. "What's wrong?"

"Honoria took a letter up to her bedchamber to read when she returned home from her visit to Whitby House, but now she refuses to come out! I can think of only one thing that would have upset her so..."

Lady Cecilia let the word trail away, but Benedict knew what she was thinking.

Honoria must have had news of her father.

He quickly peeled off his gloves and handed them with his hat to a waiting footman. "Perhaps she will speak to me."

Lady Cecilia waited for the footman to make his exit before stepping closer to Benedict and lowering her voice. "I'm more concerned about her well-being than I am about propriety, Mr. Grey. If she will admit you, don't hesitate to enter."

Benedict nodded sharply and headed up the stairs, knocking softly when he reached the closed door of Honoria's bedchamber. When the first knock brought no response, he tried again, with a little more force.

"Honoria, it's Benedict."

He heard a slight rustling before the door was whipped open. "I thought you'd never come."

There were no tear stains on her face, no puffy eyes, no signs at all that she'd been crying. She was a strong woman, but her father's death would certainly have brought intense emotion. What was going on?

She reached for his hand and pulled him into the room, shutting the door hastily behind her and marching over to her bed. "I've had a letter from my father."

He followed her part of the way. "Your aunt suspected as much. How bad is it?"

"Oh, Benedict, that's just it—it isn't bad at all." She took up the folded paper that was lying haphazardly on a brilliant blue counterpane. "The letter is in his own hand, a *steady* hand."

Benedict's brows rose as he strode the rest of the way across the room. "What does it say?"

Her dark eyes lifted to his. "He is recovering."

Chapter 6

"THAT'S WONDERFUL!" BENEDICT WRAPPED HIS arms around her and lifted her off the ground. The scent of her perfume clung to her skin and he finally placed the fragrance—apple blossoms, like those in the orchard they used to frequent before he went away.

Her hands came down on his shoulders, accompanied by a joyful laugh. "It is! It's beyond wonderful!"

Honoria's momentum carried her back to the ground, but Benedict kept her clasped against him. "There's something else, too, isn't there?

She nodded, the motion setting her curls brushing against the lapel of his coat. "He says that he's recovered enough to come to Town. He cannot participate in the activities of the

Season, of course, and he'll have to make the trip in easy stages. But he is coming here."

"It will be good to see His Grace again."

"It will. Oh it will! I thought never to see him again when I left him last." Her smile faded as her hands slid down his chest, pushing herself gently away. "But our plan..."

"Oh. Yes. We are in a bit of a situation now, aren't we?" He helped her up onto the bed and settled himself beside her, mentally sorting through their circumstances. "Well, I believe we have a few options."

"We do?"

He nodded, taking her hand in his. "We could continue on with our plan as you originally conceived it, though perhaps we no longer need the betrothal. We'll maintain our sham courtship and keep working on my dancing and deportment. If your father won't be going out, he won't be privy to gossip. Nor will he know how much time we spend together outside this house unless you or I or your aunt tells him."

"I'd have to have a conversation with Aunt Cecilia." She shifted her hand, nestling her palm snugly against his. "But Papa will be suspicious of your daily visits even if he knows nothing of our time together elsewhere. We were much together before you went to Greece, but that was several years ago. And I'm supposed to have been husband hunting these past weeks."

"You think he'll come to the conclusion all on his own that I'm courting you."

"I do." Her grip on his hand became tighter. "And he'll be so far beyond disappointment when we aren't actually wed that I think it might break his heart."

Which would be bad enough by itself. What if such distress had ill effects on His Grace's already uncertain health as well?

"We could end the ruse now. It's earlier than we had planned but you were always going to throw me over anyway."

She tucked a curl behind one ear. "Do you think you're polished enough to go the rest of the Season alone?"

"It would undoubtedly be easier with your help," he said, running his thumb across the back of her hand. "But I could manage. I suspect there are some ladies out there who like a little shyness in a gentleman."

Honoria grinned. "Oh, there definitely are such ladies. It's endearing when a gentleman summons up all his courage just for you, even when it's only to ask for a dance."

"If I could find but one that suited me, I'll have attained my goal. And my dancing has improved—I can waltz as well as anyone."

"You can." Her gaze drifted away from his, a little unfocused. "And your country dance figures are passable."

"The rest of the dances I can just sit out. Or take a turn about the room with a lady."

Her fingers loosened around his hand. "As long as you don't take her out onto the terrace alone."

"I would never do so—unless it was the lady's idea." He winked, but she wasn't looking. What was buzzing around in that head of hers? "There's another option to consider. We could truly become betrothed."

Her eyes flew back to his and her mouth formed a little O—he'd startled her with those words. Well, blast it, he'd startled himself, too. Certainly he'd been thinking about it, but he hadn't intended to address the subject like this.

"It would solve all of our problems," he explained, wondering if he was trying to convince her or himself. "I would have a wife perfectly suited to become the next Marchioness of Whitby, and you would have a husband to take care of you." She opened her mouth to speak, but Benedict held up his free hand to stop her. "I know that His Grace is on the mend, but I also know that he'll still be adamant you find a husband. He survived this last bout of illness, but he may not survive the next."

"You're probably right about that," she conceded. "I can hear him now, cajoling me to 'see reason' as he always puts it."

"His reasoning isn't wrong, you know."

She ran her free hand down the material of her skirt. "Perhaps someday a world will exist where a female does not need the protection of a husband—or anybody else—if she doesn't want it. And I know that our world isn't so, but..."

Her hand reached her knee and she lifted it to repeat the motion, but Benedict caught it in his. "But what?"

She sighed and let her eyes drop to his shoulder. "But I wanted to marry for love. This is my eleventh Season, Benedict, and I've only encountered gentlemen who were chiefly interested in my dowry or my bloodline. How are two people supposed to build a life together when one is no better than a prized mare?"

"Do you think that's how I see you? As a means to money or a link to the Maitland family tree?"

She shook her head, but still didn't meet his gaze. "To you I am Honoria: friend, dancing master, partner in verb conjugation—"

"—kisser of gentlemen in darkened front halls."

She blushed then, and Benedict watched with fascination as the color blossomed in her cheeks. When was the last time he'd seen her blush?

"I-I didn't think—"

"You always were somewhat impulsive. It got you into trouble sometimes when we were children, but I have always admired that about you."

"You have?"

He released one of her hands to grasp her chin, carefully turning her head so he could see her into eyes again. "I over-think things much of the time, and therefore am often slow to act. Your spontaneity helps me get out of my own head and experience things instead of just contemplating them."

"So you're glad I kissed you?"

He could see the beginnings of a smile tugging at the corners of her mouth and allowed his own smile to grow. "I am. If you hadn't, I'd quite possibly still be deciding if it was a good idea to try." He released her chin and inched closer to her on the bed. "Did you like kissing me?"

Her blush deepened, but she answered in a steady voice. "Yes. I don't think I did it very well, but it was pleasurable."

"If we were wed, I could teach you how it's done...and more." He was grinning fully now—he'd always enjoyed teasing her. "I do owe you for the dancing lessons."

He stood abruptly, clasping both her hands and drawing her to her feet. When he dropped to one knee, her eyes went wide. "Benedict, are you really asking me to marry you?"

"I am. We are good together, you and I, and good *for* each other. There is no other woman I'd rather have by my side. Honoria Maitland, will you do me the great honor of becoming my wife?"

She stood looking down on him, her face a mask of surprise. Benedict had surprised himself once again—he certainly hadn't planned on proposing marriage to anyone today—but this time it was a good surprise. Holding Honoria's hands in his, imagining her presiding over his home and his children, felt so very right. She'd been his best friend since they were eight years old, and he wanted to be with her always.

But she hesitated.

"Honoria?"

"Yes?"

Benedict's brows drew together. "Was that a yes, you'll marry me? Or yes, Honoria is your name."

"The second one."

Her voice was quiet, giving no indication of her feelings, and he began to feel ridiculous down on the floor at her feet. He stood with as much dignity as he could muster and rubbed his thumbs over both her hands.

"Honoria, what is it? If I've horribly mangled this proposal, I'm very, *very* sorry. I've never asked a woman for her hand before..."

Her lips twitched in a brief, sympathetic smile. "No, it isn't that. Your speech was actually quite nice."

"Then what? Whatever it is you can tell me."

She squeezed his hands and looked him straight in the eyes. "Do you love me, Benedict?"

"What?"

"I told you I wanted to marry for love, so I'm asking if you love me."

A question he'd been asking himself and for which he still had no definitive answer. "If you want to marry for love, I should be asking if *you* love *me*."

And that was apparently not the answer she was looking for. She pulled her hands from his and moved a few steps from him, taking the apple blossom scent with her. "Don't do that—don't deflect, or get pedantic. Just answer the question."

"I care about you more than anyone else." That was true, had always been true. "And there is clearly a physical attraction between us." Also true, so much that it took every ounce of self-control he possessed not to go to her, take her in his arms, and teach her more about kissing.

Her back was to him and he couldn't see her face, but her voice was flat. "But you don't love me."

"I don't know what that kind of love is, Honoria—I've never been in love before. I could love you like no other person in the world ever could and not be sure of it. Isn't my respect and affection enough?"

She was still for several agonizing moments, and Benedict finally understood her annoyances with his own long silences. How maddening it was to wait for someone to answer a simple question!

But this question was far beyond simple.

"No." Her voice was so soft he wasn't sure she'd even spoken aloud until she repeated the word. "No. It's not enough." She turned to face him but didn't approach, wrapping her arms around herself as if she were cold. "I want love,

Benedict. Real, strong, can't-mistake-it-for-anything-else love. I want to be the center of my husband's world, and for him to be the center of mine."

He ventured a step toward her. "I would make you the center of my world—you practically are already."

"Because you need me right now. You need me with you to navigate the ocean of Polite Society, to teach you to dance, to help you say the right things to the right people. Once you're wed, I doubt you'll go out much and you won't need me anymore."

He took another step. "I will always need you."

She stepped backward. "You managed for six years in Athens without me."

What could he say to that? He *had* managed without her those years, quite well in fact. He'd run Lord Elgin's entire operation without the slightest bit of help from Honoria. And it was entirely possible that he'd be off on another project in the not too distant future. Would he need her then?

His lack of answer must have ended the discussion for her, because she unwrapped one arm from her torso and pointed toward her bedchamber door. "You should go."

What? She was throwing him out? "Honoria—"

Her voice was as flat as her expression, but she was firm. "No, Benedict. I will not marry you. Our business is concluded, and you should go now."

There was certainly no use in trying to argue with the lady when he had no argument she would accept, so he bowed low and left her, not even stopping to collect his hat and gloves on the way out of the house.

Honoria remained standing, statute-like, staring at the empty doorway of her bedchamber. When Benedict asked her to marry him, she had for a moment envisioned herself as mistress of his modest house and mother of his children. She'd remembered the tender way he'd kissed her after the Philharmonic Society concert, and how wonderful it felt when he touched her. But when he couldn't tell her he loved her, she knew she couldn't go through with it.

Her father would chide her, perhaps even scold her. He would say that Benedict was her perfect match in every way, and she was daft to refuse him. But she didn't regret her decision— she wanted a man who loved her and would not settle for less.

Yet tears began welling in her eyes and she wrapped her arms tighter around herself. Would their friendship survive this day? Most certainly the answer was no. Even short formal encounters at *ton* events would be awkward now; there was no way they'd ever be comfortable enough with each other to sit together and share confidences. Nor likely would they drive or walk or dance together again, and Honoria felt a physical pain in her chest at the realization. Benedict said he'd admired her spontaneity, but this time it cost her dearly.

Chapter 7

HE MISSED HER.

> *O Venus, beauty of the skies,*
> *To whom a thousand temples rise,*
> *Gaily false in gentle smiles,*
> *Full of love-perplexing wiles;*
> *O goddess, from my heart remove*
> *The wasting cares and pains of love.*

It had been three days since Benedict's proposal—three days that he'd spent in his library, trying to find solace in books. It was a technique that had worked countless times before, quelling homesickness when he went off to Eton and later to Cambridge, helping him escape from and work through the grief at his father's death, calming his fears each time he boarded a ship and sailed away from safe, stable land.

But his books brought him no comfort this time.

It didn't help that, in an effort to drown his misery in all things ancient, he'd stumbled across a slim volume of Greek poetry. Unable to concentrate sufficiently on the foreign words, he'd distracted himself by hunting for an English translation.

Then he sat down to read it.

> *If ever thou hast kindly heard*
> *A song in soft distress preferred,*
> *Propitious to my tuneful vow,*
> *O gentle goddess, hear me now.*

Who knew a person could hurt another person so badly with one single word? Had Honoria said "yes", he would be making preparations to marry the one person in the world who had always understood him. But she'd said "no", and his whole world had fallen apart—just when he was beginning to settle into it.

Celestial visitant, once more
Thy needful presence I implore.
In pity come, and ease my grief,
Bring my distempered soul relief

Grief was—surprisingly—the very word to describe his emotional state. He *was* grieving, not for the loss of a comfortable marriage but for the loss of his closest friend, only weeks after they'd found each other again. How would he manage without her?

Honoria had insisted that he got by in Athens without a whit of support from her, but he realized that she was wrong. She might not have been with him, but she had frequently been in his thoughts. Most of the letters he'd received from his mother had included scraps of news pertaining to Honoria. Often they were frivolous things, like the color of her new dress or the way she'd styled her hair. Sometimes there were more serious anecdotes: how she'd sat with her father when he was ill or how capably she handled the household. Whatever the tidings, they always brought a sense of warmth and affection and home.

Favour thy suppliant's hidden fires,
And give me all my heart desires.

He buried his face in the pages of the book. "I am an idiot."

"We're all a little slow sometimes, cousin."

Benedict straightened to find Whitby standing alone at the door of the library. "How the devil did you get in here?"

Whitby strode to one of the windows and threw back the closed curtains, ignoring the question. "Lady Whitby and I were worried when you failed to turn up for Eleanor's come-out last night."

"What? Oh, right—your eldest's ball. That was last night?"

Whitby went to the other window and dragged open those curtains as well, allowing harsh sunlight to flood the room. "It was. And you disappointed her severely." He turned to face his cousin. "When I arrived here to see what had happened to you, your valet and butler said you were in a sorry state—holed up here with your books, not speaking to anyone, having to be coaxed to bed at night, not eating or sleeping much. You look like hell, too. Have you been drinking?"

Benedict ran a hand over the beard sprouting on his face. How long had it been since he'd shaved? "No."

Whitby dropped into his favorite chair. "Maybe you should. What happened?"

"I asked Honoria to marry me."

Whitby rose and went to the sideboard, pouring out two measures of ouzo from the decanter. He didn't say anything until he'd brought one glass to Benedict and returned to his chair. "That explains your new title—are you Baron Idiot, Viscount Idiot, or something a bit higher up?"

"I believe you may have to start calling me Your Grace." Benedict looked at the glass, then set it on the small table beside him.

Whitby winced. "Ouch. Do you want to talk about it? Or do you want to sit here and brood some more? I'm game for either, but I'm not leaving you alone like this."

"Ironically, this is something I would have talked to Honoria about—especially before I went to Athens. Even when I was at university we remained close."

"But now?"

"But now I suspect she never wants to see me again."

"What did you do?"

Benedict hung his head. "She asked me if I loved her...and I hedged."

"That doesn't sound so bad."

"But it was." Benedict planted his elbows on his knees and dropped his head into his hands. "She told me she wanted to marry for love, Whitby. Then she asked me if I loved her, and I didn't say yes."

Whitby sat back in his chair and whistled. "You *are* an idiot, then. Anyone who's been within a mile of you two knows you're in love with her."

Benedict's hands scrubbed through his tangled hair. "Well, I didn't figure that out until today."

"And if you explain that to her now, it will look like you're telling her what she wants to hear to get her to the altar."

"Precisely."

Whitby grinned. "Did I ever tell you how many times I proposed before Lady Whitby accepted? It was four. Four times I asked her for her hand, and four times she turned me down. I don't even remember the reasons she gave—you'll have to ask her, she tells the story better than I do—but she damn near broke my heart each time. I almost didn't try again, but I'd discovered that life was invariably sweeter when I was with her. And there's that stubborn streak that runs in the family, too—I had to try one more time."

"I'm not asking for Honoria's hand five times, cousin."

Whitby's grin turned into a laugh. "You will if she keeps turning you down."

Benedict groaned. "How did you even find the courage to talk to her again? Or to go out in public when the whole of the *ton* knew what happened?"

Whitby's expression faded into something more serious. "I knew she was worth it. I didn't care what I had to go through, I just needed her with me."

Benedict blew out a heavy sigh. "I do love her, but I don't know if I can handle another rejection."

"You've not recovered yet from this one," Whitby said, rising from his chair and ambling the few steps to his cousin. He clapped a hand on Benedict's shoulder and gave it a squeeze. "Take some more time with Homer, or whatever you're reading. Drink some ouzo, or whisky, or lemonade if it makes you feel better. When you're ready, try again."

"It's Sappho. And next time I'll have a solid plan."

"That's the spirit," Whitby smiled, giving his cousin another pat. "A better plan gives you a better chance."

"That explains this disaster, then—I had no plan at all."

Whitby returned to his chair, his eyes and mouth wide with exaggerated horror. "No plan? No wonder she refused you."

"Shut up." Benedict rubbed his hands over his face. "You know I have no improvisational skills. I didn't intend to ask her to be my wife that day, it just sort of happened. And I've never been good with 'just sort of happened'."

"True, but you're more at ease with people you know well. And you know Lady Honoria better than just about anybody. Don't over-think it."

"Good advice," Benedict said, reaching for his abandoned glass of ouzo. "You know me rather well, too."

"He's here."

Honoria walked into the enormous ballroom at Almack's with her Aunt, her eyes instinctively roaming the crowd of people—as they had for the past week—looking for Benedict. He topped most men by two or three inches, making him easy to spot even among a sea of gentlemen wearing similar dark tailcoats. Whether she wanted to seek him out or avoid him, she didn't know. Nor had it mattered—she'd seen not a whisper of him since she refused him and ordered him from her home.

Until now. To her surprise she found him here in the Assembly Rooms, not in the throng of onlookers but in the midst of the dancers. He was partnering a girl—and a girl she was, looking as though she still belonged in the schoolroom—only a few inches shorter than he was in a country dance. Her chestnut hair glinted in the light from the candles in the chandeliers above, her white gown swirling about her as she moved.

"Who is here?" Aunt Cecilia asked, trying to follow her niece's gaze.

"Benedict. And he's *dancing*."

Aunt Cecilia craned her neck, heedless of decorum. "He is—and doing it rather well. You should be proud of your pupil, my dear."

"Who is that he's with? I don't recognize her."

"I don't either. She must be a new debutante." Aunt Cecilia tilted her head slightly. "He seems to be enjoying her company, whoever she is."

Drat the man, he did seem so. His face was animated when he spoke to his partner between figures of the dance, and when he wasn't speaking he was smiling.

He had never looked that merry during his lessons with Honoria.

She shook off the thought, and the feeling of discontent that it brought. What did it matter to her who Benedict danced with? She had no claim on him.

"Well, good for him," she managed. And a part of her *was* truly happy to see him so much at ease in public—it had simply never occurred to her that he could be so with someone else.

Another part of her, though, longed to be the one he smiled at, the one who took his arm as he led her from the dance floor. She wanted his hazel eyes to light up when they saw her, and to be swept up in his arms and kissed witless. She wanted to share confidences and opinions and plans and...

And she had said no when he offered it all to her.

"Aunt Cecilia, might we return home? I'm suddenly not feeling very well."

"Are you certain? We've only just arrived." Her aunt turned toward her and put a hand to Honoria's cheek. "You do look a bit pale. Perhaps some lemonade and a dance would help?"

Honoria shook her head. "If I wasn't feeling ill, that awful lemonade would surely make me so. And I don't feel like dancing."

Aunt Cecilia's eyes widened. "You must feel poorly indeed. I'll call for the carriage."

They waited together near the entrance, Honoria hooking her arm through her aunt's and holding it more tightly than she meant to.

By the time the carriage arrived, Aunt Cecilia looked genuinely worried, seating herself beside her niece and wrapping an arm around Honoria's shoulders.

"It's Mr. Grey, isn't it?" she asked softly.

Honoria laid her head on her aunt's shoulder. "I am a fool. A blind fool. It was never supposed to turn out this way."

"Things rarely end up the way we plan them."

"Nearly everything did this time—but that's the problem."

Aunt Cecilia gave Honoria's shoulders a little squeeze. "What happened?"

"You know about the promise I made to Papa when he thought he was dying. Well, I didn't want to marry just anyone. In fact, I didn't want to marry anyone at all unless he loved me."

"Not an easy thing to do."

Honoria shook her head. "Then I ran into Benedict at Lady Whitby's ball." She smiled in the darkness of the carriage, recalling how literal that statement was. "He needed help polishing his society manners, and I offered him a bargain. I'd teach him to dance and make himself agreeable, and he would act as if he were courting me. We were going to announce a betrothal for Papa's sake, then I was going to cry off after..."

Aunt Cecilia nodded against the crown of Honoria's head. "But your father recovered."

"And Benedict asked for my hand—a real offer, not the subterfuge I'd concocted. I-I sent him away."

"That was the day your father's letter arrived. I wondered why Mr. Grey left without so much as a word."

Honoria turned her face toward her aunt's silken sleeve. "I refused him. He couldn't tell me he loved me so I refused him."

"Then you saw him with another lady tonight."

Honoria lifted her head from Aunt Cecilia's shoulder and snorted indelicately. "Lady? She was half my age if she was a day. What can she give him that I cannot?"

"A 'yes'."

Honoria frowned in the dark. "I deserved that."

"It's true." Aunt Cecilia found Honoria's hand and clasped it in hers. "And you have a decision to make. You can make up your mind to let Mr. Grey go on to whatever happiness he might find without you. Or you can float along like a paper boat on the Serpentine and wait to see if he comes back to you."

"But he was never really mine to begin with. It was all for show."

"Was it?"

Was it? Had Honoria missed something her aunt had seen? "Or?"

"Or," Aunt Cecilia continued, "you can play an active part in your future."

Honoria gestured with her free hand, even though she knew her aunt couldn't see her do it. "I tried that, and look how it turned out."

"You did try—once. The question is, are you going to try again?"

Honoria had no ready answer, and leaned against Aunt Cecilia for physical support as well as the emotional kind. "What would you do?"

Aunt Cecilia put both her arms around her niece and hugged her. "It doesn't matter what I would do. It only matters what you will do."

Honoria bid her aunt good night and went to her bedchamber as soon as they reached Alston House. What *would* she do? There wasn't a passive bone in her body, she was certain of that. But when she had tried to take her future in hand, she'd made a complete mess of her oldest friendship. And she loved Benedict, despite his own ambiguity. If she went to him and an agreement was struck, could she spend the rest of her life with a man who very possibly didn't love her in return? Was she settling to try to soothe her heart?

If she let him go, she knew there would be more nights like this one. He would eventually find a woman who was satisfied with his affection and respect. Honoria would see them together when they came to Town for the Season—if they came to Town. Perhaps Benedict would find a lady who was content to spend her days in the country, or the museums. Or one who would travel with him to excavation sites all over the world. She'd never see them together in those cases.

She'd never see him at all.

Chapter 8

$\mathscr{B}$ENEDICT STOOD IN THE MORNING room of his townhouse, staring at a potted sapling sitting in the middle of the breakfast table—a cutting from an apple tree that lived in the orchard he and Honoria used to frequent. He had sent for it the same day he sent the note to Honoria pledging his participation in her pretend courtship, and it had arrived this afternoon. He'd meant it as a gift to her, thinking a reminder of the good times they'd shared would be comforting when her father was so ill.

What was he going to do with it now?

A footman stepped tentatively through the open door. "Lady Honoria Maitland has arrived, sir."

What? She was in his house? "I'll see her here."

The footman bowed himself out and Benedict combed his fingers through his hair. A thousand reasons for Honoria's visit ran through his head as he straightened his cravat and waistcoat. Was it her father? Had some evil befallen him on his journey to Town? Had one of her suitors offered for her? Had her aunt fallen ill? He hadn't put on a tailcoat this morning. Did he have time to do it now?

"Hello, Benedict."

She stood alone in the doorway, clothed in a pinkish dress with little flowers embroidered all over it and looking as beautiful as he'd ever seen her. Her bonnet was still tied securely under her chin, though, and the brim shaded her face enough to keep her expression a mystery.

At least she had called him Benedict, not Mr. Grey. "Hello, Honoria. Your maid can wait in the kitchen if she chooses. I don't have much in the way of staff, but she'll find some company there."

"I didn't bring a maid."

His brows drew together. "You didn't come here alone...did you?"

She nodded, making the silk rose on her bonnet flutter. "I took a hackney so no one would see the Alston crest on the carriage."

"You don't think my neighbors may have seen you at the door?" He reached for her arm and tugged her into the room. "You've all but ruined your reputation."

"I don't care. I needed to talk to you."

She would care one if the gossip rags got wind of this. "Very well. But take off your hat—I'll not have a conversation with half your face."

He pulled out a chair from the breakfast table and she sat, carefully pulling her bonnet off. When she began to pluck her gloves from her fingers, he seated himself beside her. But she didn't speak. She kept her eyes on her hands as if her gloves were dangerous items that might go off at any moment.

But he could not take the silence. He turned himself sideways in his chair and leaned forward, inelegantly pulling her gloves off and depositing them on the table where she'd placed her bonnet. The faint scent of apple blossoms clung to her skin. "Now, what would you like to talk about?"

Her eyes remained focused on her hands. "I-I don't know. I didn't get that far in my plan."

He couldn't help but smile. "You risked being compromised—rendered unmarriageable and unfit for society—to come here, but you don't know what you wanted to say?"

She raised her eyes to his, one brow arched with a touch of defiance. "I did."

Oh, did he love her! How could he have ever doubted it? "Why don't we talk about this specimen on my table then?"

"All right."

Her uncertainty seemed to bolster his confidence, and he took both her hands in his. "Do you remember the spring you father and stepmother were wed?"

"I do. Papa insisted we have the wedding at Orchard Lake and turned it into a week-long fête."

Honoria wrinkled her nose, and Benedict laughed. "You liked that estate best out of all His Grace's properties. Don't pretend you didn't."

"I didn't like being dragged back into the country in the middle of my second Season."

The expression on her face softened. "You came down from Cambridge for the ceremony."

"Mmhmm. I stayed at Whitby's Westbrook next door. Remember?"

She was leaning slightly forward now, a small smile on her lips. "Half the *ton* came, too, so I got to finish my Season after all. Papa hired that orchestra to play in the little folly behind the house, and we danced outdoors until it was too dark to see. Except when we'd sneak off to the orchard and read when the crowd got to be too much for you."

"*I* used to read," he grinned. "You would sit beside me on the blanket and talk about your beaux, your dresses, the dresses other girls had worn, your new stepmother, how happy your father looked, the weather—"

She freed one of her hands to smack his knee. "I didn't talk that much." Her fingers slid back into his grasp. "Did I?"

"Yes, you did. But I didn't mind. I liked being there with you, having you close to me."

"I liked spending that time with you, too. But what does that have to do with this?" She nodded toward the sapling.

Benedict released her hands and rose from his chair, bending across the table to grab hold of the pot and drag it closer. "We always sat near that enormous apple tree—"

"The one that seemed to have more blossoms on it than the others, every single year. It smelled heavenly."

"Is that why you wear apple blossom perfume?" he asked, allowing himself to be diverted for a moment. It was a question he'd been meaning to ask her.

A pink tinge crept into her cheeks. "I only started wearing that a few weeks ago. I-I noticed your applewood scent during one of our dancing lessons..."

A fluttery sensation flooded Benedict's body and he felt giddy. She wore apple blossom perfume because he wore applewood, and had risked her future with the *beau monde* to talk to him alone.

"Do you know why I chose applewood?"

"I figured it had to do with our orchard."

Our orchard. How right she was. "That spring in the orchard? I think that's when I fell in love with you." He pushed his chair back with one foot and knelt before her, clasping her hands in his once more. "And I have loved you with all my heart every since. I was just too addle-pated to know it."

Honoria laughed—a bright, bubbly laugh that sounded like a hundred years worth of happiness in one burst. "I'm afraid I was just as slow as you were, my love. But the important thing is that we get it right at some point in time."

"I believe that point is now." He brushed his lips over the backs of her hands. "I will never be comfortable in society, never enjoy it the way you do. But if you will always save me a dance and sit with me in the orchard, I'll find a way to manage. I love you too much to do otherwise. Will you marry me, Honoria?"

She jumped from her chair and pulled him to his feet, throwing her arms around his neck. "Yes!"

His arms slid around her and held her against him as she lifted her face for a kiss.

He didn't disappoint her.

"Oh my goodness, your mother was right..."

Honoria was nestled snugly beside her betrothed on a sofa in his library, his arm wrapped securely around her. They'd migrated there from the morning room wanting to be more comfortable than the breakfast table allowed, knowing all the while that Honoria should return home as soon as possible. But Benedict's fingers slowly stroking her arm turned "as soon as possible" into just "soon". When she dropped a soft kiss on his jaw and laid her head against his shoulder, he declared that an hour together wouldn't do any harm.

"What was my mother right about?"

Her fingers toyed with the buttons of his waistcoat. "When I visited Whitby House, she said she though you and I had fallen in love before you went to Greece. I told her she was mistaken, but she wouldn't be dissuaded."

"She saw it before we did."

"Or it was wishful thinking," she replied. "You had been away at university, and I'd had a few Seasons—we weren't in each other's company as much in those days."

He kissed her hair. "Either way Mother will be happy."

Honoria sat up, bracing a hand against his chest. "What about you? Are you happy? Truly?"

"Yes," he said, brushing a finger against her cheek. "Can you not tell?"

He had a silly smile plastered on his face and she grinned. "To be sure."

"What about you? Are you happy?"

"It just hasn't sunk in yet, I think." She settled back against him, taking one of his hands in hers and drawing his arm around her. "I made the decision to marry for love during my first Season, and that was quite a while ago."

"And I'm enormously glad of it. I could not imagine myself leg-shackled to a girl ten years my junior. Plenty of gentleman do it, but I was looking for a wife I could partner, not one I had to raise."

That triggered a memory from her brief sojourn at the Assembly Rooms. "Then who was that you were dancing with at Almack's last night? She looked rather on the young side."

"Why, Lady Honoria, are you jealous?"

She felt his chuckle vibrate through her. "Yes, you cursed man, I am." There was heat in her voice, but his amusement was fueling her own as well. "Who was she?"

"My cousin, Eleanor."

She sat up again, releasing his hand and turning herself all the way around to look at him. "Your cousin?"

"Whitby's daughter, the oldest. I was supposed to lead her out for the opening set at her debutante ball, but I was so aggrieved by your refusal that I forgot about the whole thing." Benedict reached for her, letting his hand glide over her skin before clasping her fingers in his. "I escorted her to Almack's to make up for it."

"How did you get in?" She frowned for a moment, realizing how discourteous her question sounded, then backtracked. "I mean, the Patronesses only grant vouches to men they are particularly fond of. I wasn't aware you knew any of them that well."

"I don't, but my mother and Lady Whitby had a word with Lady Castlereagh." His mouth pulled into a grin. "They assured her that my dancing would be impeccable."

Honoria gave him a sly smile. "Too bad Almack's doesn't allow the waltz."

"Better that they don't," he replied. "You are the only woman I've ever waltzed with, and I prefer to keep it that way."

He leaned in and kissed her then, one hand resting on her hip while the other threaded through her hair, scattering pins on the sofa cushions. Aunt Cecilia would notice the difference in Honoria's appearance when she returned home, even after everything was set to rights, but Honoria didn't care. Her arms went around Benedict and she held him close, breaking away to press her lips to his cheek, his temple, his jaw.

"I prefer it that way, too," she murmured. "You will be my 'only' for many things—I'm glad I can be yours for at least one."

"Oh, more than one," he corrected, planting a final kiss on the tip of her nose. "You're also the only woman I ever got drunk with, or learned dead languages with. And the only woman I think of when I smell apple blossoms.

She set her forearms on his shoulders and pushed back to look into his eyes. "Is that what the tree is for in your morning room?"

"It is now." His arms slipped around her waist and held her firmly. "It was originally going to be a gift for you—a cutting from our favorite tree at Orchard Lake."

"Perhaps we can plant it in the garden."

"Here? I thought you'd prefer a larger home."

She let her fingers wander lightly through his hair. "I will prefer any home you happen to be in."

His eyes closed for a moment as his entire face relaxed. "I'll show you the rest before I take you back to your aunt. You can tell me then if you think the nursery is large enough."

She brushed her lips across his cheek. "Are we going to have so many children, then?"

He opened his eyes and she could see flecks of gold and green in his irises. "We must at least try. I am the last Grey male. And there's another 'only': you'll be the only Mrs. Benedict Grey."

"Unless I am Lady Honoria Grey," she reminded him with a smirk. "I can do that, you know."

He slid a hand slowly up her back. "I do know. And I don't care which title you use—as long as it's my name you have and my life you share."

She smiled and drew him closer for another kiss. "Every blessed minute of it."

Epilogue

August 1815

THE HOUSE WAS QUIET WHEN Honoria entered, in direct opposition to the chaos that had reigned when she left. It was dark, too, except for the candle carried by the butler in the entry.

"Good evening, madam."

"Good evening. Is my husband still up?"

"He retired to the master bedchamber some hours ago, madam. Whether he is still awake or not, I cannot say."

She smiled. "Hopefully he didn't fall asleep reading again, with the candles still burning. And Emily?"

"Sleeping peacefully in the nursery."

He offered to light her way upstairs but she declined, sending him off to bed and climbing the stairs in the darkness. In the two years she'd been mistress of this house she'd come to know all its secrets, and could find her way around blindfolded.

After a stop in the nursery to check on her sleeping child, she reached the chamber she shared with Benedict and gently pushed the door open, peeping through the widening space to see if he slept as soundly as his daughter did.

"Ah, the prodigal wife returns."

He was reclining on the big bed clad only in breeches and shirt, with a book in his lap, as Honoria had predicted, but far from sleeping. He slid off the counterpane and met her halfway across the room, wrapping his arms around her despite the summer heat.

"Welcome home." He bent down and kissed her softly, then kissed her again with more eagerness, as if she had been gone days rather than hours. "I missed you."

"I missed you, too," she replied, rising up on her toes to drape her own arms around his neck.

"How was the ball?"

"Lady Lambert outdid herself this year—every inch of the house was decorated in roses, and she had seven kinds of cake."

He laughed. "Seven? Perhaps I should have gone after all."

"You would have been bored," she told him, massaging his nape. "I nearly was myself some of the time."

"What about your aunt?"

Honoria grinned. "My aunt is so besotted with her new husband she scarcely noticed anything else."

"Hmm, sounds like someone else I know." He planted a big, smacking kiss on her cheek.

She pushed him playfully away. "We are not newly wed anymore."

"But you are still besotted with me."

She liked how he stated rather than asked it. "Yes, I am."

"As I am with you." He brushed his lips against her forehead.

She savored his embrace, but all too quickly the high temperature intruded. "Will you help me out of this gown? If I wear it any longer I fear I'll melt into a puddle at your feet."

He arched a suggestive eyebrow at her, but turned her by the shoulders and went methodically to work on her laces.

"How is the packing coming?" she asked over her shoulder.

She felt the tugging stop for a moment.

"I don't remember having this much to do before I left for Greece."

"You didn't have a wife and daughter to cart with you then." The tugging resumed and moments later Honoria's bodice fell from her shoulders. She stepped carefully out of the gown, laying it over a chair to deal with later.

He pressed a kiss to the back of her neck and began unlacing her stays. "That must be it."

"You're sure you want to take us all the way to Italy?" She'd probably asked him the same question a dozen times in the last month as their departure date drew nearer. "You'd be able to inspect the work done at the Forum much more easily without us."

Her stays peeled off her body and slid to her feet, and he kissed her shoulder. "You know I would expire of wanting the both of you before I ever even crossed the Channel."

She kicked away the corset and plopped down in a chair to remove her shoes and stockings. "Then I fear your baggage train will be disproportionately large."

"I don't care if we have to commission a special ship to carry it all," he smiled. "But it won't be that bad. I had a letter from Mother today—she's arrived safely in Rome and has found us a house. By the time we get there, it will be furnished and staffed. The largest of our trunks are going tomorrow, so they should be there before us, too."

"Good."

He took both her hands and pulled her to her feet. "Dance with me. We'll imagine we're in Lady Lambert's lavish ballroom, with the orchestra playing whatever we want them to play, and forget about trying to move our household across an entire continent."

Dressed now only in her shift, she grasped his upper arm with her left hand, laying her right hand on his offered palm as his free arm came around her. "We cannot dance this close together in public, my love. It's unseemly."

He grinned and drew her even more snugly against him, waltzing her slowly around the room. "Then forget the ballroom. It's just the two of us, here in our bedchamber."

She closed her eyes and nestled her head against his chest. "That is exactly what I want."

His lips pressed against her hair once, twice, before he spoke again. "Then it's exactly what you shall always have."

Ready for more Maitland Maidens? Read on for a sneak peek...

Back In My Arms Again

Maitland Maidens Book 2

Chapter 1

JAMES FITZSIMMONS SAT BEFORE THE fireplace in his best friend's drawing room, staring at the letters in his lap. There were three, each promising ruination and even imprisonment to the recipient should certain conditions not be met by Lady Day—the twenty-fifth of March— namely that a loan totaling the princely sum of three thousand pounds be paid in full.

The sender was the powerful Earl of Grimsby. The recipient was James's father.

"How am I going to come up with three thousand pounds in six weeks?"

Stephen Eddington settled himself on a sofa set at a right angle to James's chair, placing his elbows on his knees and resting his chin in his hands. "Well, you can't borrow against the farm."

James's father had done precisely that, igniting the fire that James was now trying to put out. "I can't ask our neighbors for help. They are comfortable, but not so wealthy they could spare this kind of money even if everyone we know contributed."

"And your father would be none too happy if they found out why he needed the money so quickly."

Because the elder Fitzsimmons had shown exceedingly poor judgment in this financial matter. Grimsby's reputation marked the earl out as deceitful and avaricious in his financial dealings, and less than gentlemanly even with the men of his own class.

James scrubbed a hand through his hair and over his face. "This would be a good time for a long-lost wealthy relative to appear and offer to make this all go away."

Eddington straightened. "That's a good idea. Not a relative, but perhaps you can find a patron who will lend you the money. I'll put up my own property as collateral if it will help."

"You're a good friend, Eddy, but I can't ask you to do that."

"You didn't ask—I volunteered," Eddington returned with a quick grin. "That, together with the ledgers from the farm for the past several years, should be enough to convince a wealthy merchant or aristocrat to lend you the three thousand pounds. Your family keeps the farm and uses some of the income from it to pay back your benefactor. No one loses their home or livelihood."

James turned the scenario over in his mind. The Fitzsimmons Farm had a long history of solid production and the documentation to prove it, so that would be an incentive to a would-be lender. It was probably the inducement his father had used to obtain the three thousand from Grimsby in the first place, though it wasn't worth that much outright. Neither was Eddington's little estate. But if they found a sympathetic ear...

"What is it?" Eddington asked, jarring James from his thoughts.

"What's what?"

"You're wrinkling your nose as if you've encountered some noxious smell. What are you thinking about that's so distasteful?"

James suppressed a sigh. "You know I don't like dealing with the aristocracy. But it appears that my family's very existence now depends on one of them."

"I did say a wealthy merchant would do as well."

"Do you know any merchants who might be willing to help?"

Eddington shook his head. "No. But I do know some aristocrats who might take pity on you."

James felt his nose wrinkle again and his mouth pull into a frown. "I don't want their pity."

"Just their money."

Ouch. But Eddy was right, and James didn't have time to be choosy. If pity was part of the bargain then he'd have to learn to live with it.

"Fine. Where do we find these soft-hearted people with large bank accounts?"

"Phillip Maitland and his wife are having a house party in a few days. They won't have the sum required, but they are well connected—Mr.

Maitland is cousin to the Duke of Alston and spent some time in the Commons as an MP."

James felt his body tense at the mention of the Maitland name and the duke's title. He'd known the duke's own sister in his youth—intimately. But it had been nearly two decades since he'd last seen her, and he highly doubted she would welcome him now.

He pushed the thought aside and tried to focus on his family's current predicament. "Can we wangle a dinner invitation one evening, do you think?"

Eddington smiled brightly. "Better. I've been invited to the house party, and Mrs. Maitland just sent a note asking if I knew another gentleman that might be available. It seems she had a last-minute cancellation and needs to even out the numbers."

James hesitated. A Maitland house party? Would Cecilia be there? "Are you sure I'll be welcome? Dinner is one thing, but an entire house party is a bit more presumptuous."

"It's only a couple of weeks. And there's bound to be someone there who can help you. Mrs. Maitland will be so glad to have an equal number of ladies and gentlemen she may even let you court her daughter."

"Two birds, one stone—how efficient. My mother would be pleased," James replied in a flat voice. She'd taken to reminding him that, while James's sister's son could inherit the farm, the boy didn't carry the Fitzsimmons name, and impressing upon James how wonderful it would be to have a grandchild that did. But Cecilia Maitland had hurt James badly the one and only time he'd proposed marriage, and at seven-and-thirty he was no longer interested in the almost political maneuverings some people undertook to make the "right" match.

"There's been no indication that Lady Cecilia will be there—she's only a distant cousin to Mr. Maitland."

James eyed his friend doubtfully. "You can't be sure of that."

Eddy shook his head. "No, I can't. But I can be sure that your farm will be in Grimsby's hands if you don't go."

"You have a point there."

"You'll go, then?"

James nodded, resigned. He could brazen out a Maitland house party in order to save the farm. And perhaps Eddy was right about Cecilia's presence there. "I'll go, and thank you for any information you can provide about the other guests."

Eddington sank back against the sofa cushions. "You're welcome to everything I know about them. Mr. and Mrs. Maitland are excellent hosts, too—you might even enjoy yourself."

James wasn't sure he'd enjoy anything until the farm was safe, but he nodded again to appease Eddington. "I might."

"You'll certainly feel better after some preparation. Come, let's adjourn to my study and we'll see what we can glean from Mrs. Maitland's invitation."

Lady Cecilia Maitland knocked on the door of her cousin's bedchamber, hoping the hour wasn't too late. Cecilia and Margaret had both been asked to arrive for the house party early to help with the preparations, and Cecilia found herself in need of counsel.

The door opened to reveal a fully-clothed Margaret Maitland, who smiled brightly when her eyes met Cecilia's. "I didn't expect to see you this late. I thought surely you'd be abed and sleeping soundly after traveling all day."

"I would be, but sleep has been rather elusive these past few nights."

Margaret took a step back and opened the door wider. "Would you like to come in for a bit? Maybe a nice chat will settle you."

"I was hoping you'd say that." Cecilia entered the room, closing her eyes momentarily to savor the heat radiating from the fireplace. There were two comfortable-looking chairs placed near the hearth, and Cecilia seated herself in the one closest to the window while Margaret took the other.

"So what has been keeping you up these past nights?"

Cecilia suppressed a smile. How very like a Maitland to get right to the point. "I've found myself in some trouble, and I'm hoping you can help me discover a way to get out of it."

Margaret's brows rose. "What kind of trouble now?"

This time Cecilia allowed the smile to form on her lips. She was the unconventional member of the Maitland family, the forty-year-old woman who set up her own household and invested her money rather than marry and depend on a husband. Being the daughter and sister of a duke meant most of the ton brushed off what they called her eccentricities, but Cecilia's society life had not been without incident.

But her smile faded as she spoke. "I have a blackmailer."

"What?"

"The Earl of Grimsby has an old letter of mine in his possession. One written to a lover many years ago that would disgrace me and the whole family if it became public. Or so he says."

Margaret sat back in her chair. "You doubt the existence of this letter?"

"I don't, actually. I vividly remember writing a number of letters to a certain gentleman when I was younger, so it's possible that Grimsby does possess one of them. Though I'll never know how he got his hands on it."

"You're worried about the effect on your reputation, then?"

Cecilia shook her head, her blonde nighttime plait sliding a little against her back. "I have position and wealth enough to withstand whatever backlash might occur, and I'm not exactly hunting for a husband. No, my concern is that my brother will find out."

His Grace the Duke of Alston was older than Cecilia by twelve years and had been in delicate health most of his adult life. Over the past few years "delicate" had been supplanted by "dreadful" more often than not, and the family knew it was only a matter of time before he went to his reward.

"You think the shock will be too much for him."

Margaret's voice was solemn and Cecilia gave a little nod, listening to the fire crackle cheerily along as if everything were fine.

"And you came to me because I'm no stranger to scandal."

Cecilia opened her mouth to protest, but saw that her cousin was smiling. Margaret had borne a child out of wedlock when she was nineteen and had withdrawn from Society as a result. Cecilia knew it had crushed Margaret to live as an exile in the country, particularly when she'd been so young and full of adventure. She didn't often refer to her status, but it was good to see her speaking so easily of it now.

"Because you're my favorite cousin," Cecilia returned.

Margaret chuckled. "Don't let Phillip hear you say that."

Cecilia wanted to grin and reply with some witty comment, but instead she pressed her lips together for a moment. "You can't tell anyone about this, including Phillip—the more people that know, the greater the chance someone will tell Alston."

Margaret reached across the space between their chairs and clasped Cecilia's hands in hers. "Of course I won't. Your secret is safe with me." She squeezed her cousin's hands then released them and sat back. "Now what can we do about Grimsby? What is it that he wants from you?"

"Five thousand pounds. For that I get the actual letter in addition to his silence."

Margaret's hazel eyes went round. "Five thousand?" Then she smiled. "If your investments are doing as well as they appear to be, that isn't an insurmountable sum for you. Is it?"

"No, it isn't. But that's not the point."

"You're angry that he's trying to manipulate you."

Margaret's tone was so matter-of-fact Cecilia grinned. "I'd forgotten just how well you know me. Yes, I'm angry that he thinks he can so easily move me. But I can't tell the magistrate what's happened for fear of word getting out, and Grimsby well knows it—is counting on it."

"Are you still in contact with the letter's original recipient? Perhaps you could write to him and let him know what is happening. He may even have an idea or two about how to stop it."

Cecilia pictured James as he'd been when she'd known him, tall and slim yet strong enough to lift her off the ground with little effort. He'd had a dimple in his left cheek—just a fraction of an inch from the corner of his mouth—that she'd been particularly fond of kissing. But it had been nearly twenty years since she'd seen him last, and the encounter had not ended happily.

"We lost touch," she told her cousin, which was a version of the truth. His actual words had been something more akin to I never want to see you again. "I suppose I could set my solicitor to searching for him, but he doesn't go about in Society."

"Then he may not care about the letter surfacing, which is just as well. I think the only thing he could really do to help is marry you. That would render the letter moot."

Cecilia nodded slowly, as if it was a simple thing Margaret suggested. Marriage to her former lover would negate the scandal the letter would otherwise cause for all but the highest sticklers, and those were people who didn't approve of her anyway. What she didn't tell Margaret was that James had been more than just a lover. He'd been a close friend, an ally, and her would-be fiancé. If Cecilia had accepted James's proposal of marriage all those years ago, she wouldn't be having this problem now.

Would she have been happier as his wife?

But what was done, was done. For all she knew, he was wed to some other woman and had a full complement of children helping him run the farm.

"Marriage to anyone would probably negate enough of the scandal that little would reach Alston, particularly if he were confined to his home or bed. I am loath to give up my independence, though, Margaret. I've been my own keeper for nigh on sixteen years now, and to sign everything over to a man feels like a defeat."

"You could retain some of your independence with the right settlements...and the right gentleman," Margaret replied with a sly smile. "And marriage would undoubtedly be more pleasurable than giving in to Grimsby."

"His lordship certainly wouldn't see it coming."

"And in a few days you'll have a house party full of gentlemen to consider."

"Half of whom I'm related to," Cecilia quipped. "But at least it's a viable action, if I want to take it. I would just have to find a willing co-conspirator."

Other Books by Cora Lee

<u>Sweet & Traditional</u>
Save the Last Dance for Me (Maitland Maidens #1)
Back In My Arms Again (Maitland Maidens #2)
Kissing by the Mistletoe (Maitland Maidens #3)
A Kiss to Build a Dream On (Maitland Maidens #4)
When I Fall In Love (Maitland Maidens #5)

<u>Spicy Novellas</u>
What If I Loved You

<u>Spicy and Suspenseful</u>
No Rest for the Wicked
The Good, The Bad, And The Scandalous
The Duke of Darkness

About the Author

Cora Lee is National Bestselling author of Regency romance. She went on a twelve year expedition through the blackboard jungle as a high school math teacher before publishing *Save the Last Dance for Me*, the first book in the Maitland Maidens series. She then followed it up with eight more novels and novellas, ranging from sweet and traditional to spicy and suspenseful.

When she's not walking Rotten Row at the fashionable hour or attending the entertainments of the Season, you might find her participating in Regency Fiction Writers events, wading through her towering TBR pile, or eagerly awaiting the next Marvel movie release. If you'd like to find out more about Cora or her books you can visit her website, sign up for her newsletter, or connect with her on Bookbub, Facebook, or Goodreads.